The
Squire's
Quest

The Squire's Quest

GERALD MORRIS

Houghton Mifflin
Houghton Mifflin Harcourt
Boston New York

To Karen Ebert,
who is real.

The text of this book is set in 12.5-point Horley Old Style.

Library of Congress Cataloging-in-Publication Data is on file.

ISBN 978-0-547-14424-5

Manufactured in the United States of America
DOC 10 9 8 7 6 5 4 3 2
4500212073

O purblind race of miserable men,
How many among us at this very hour
Do forge a life-long trouble for ourselves,
By taking true for false, or false for true . . .

—Alfred Lord Tennyson,
Idylls of the King

Contents

BOOK I:
ALEXANDER

1

TERENCE AND EILEEN

Terence gazed glumly from the turret of Camelot's highest tower. Before his eyes lay miles of tidy patch-work farms, bordered by hedgerows and forests, all tied together by ribbons of well-kept roads. Britain under King Arthur was a picture of tranquility, a picture that was belied by the tense, anxious emptiness that Terence had felt growing within for more than a month. He turned and picked his way down the tower's winding stairs.

At ground level, Terence crossed a courtyard where young squires practiced swordplay with wooden cudgels. He nodded to them and returned several polite greetings: although he was older than the next oldest squire present by at least ten years, he was still one of them, in the service of King Arthur's nephew Gawain.

He stopped once to offer advice to a young squire who was scrubbing at a spot of rust on a breastplate, then continued through the court to the chambers that he shared with Gawain. Gawain sat in an armchair by the fire, nursing a pot of ale.

"There you are, lad," Gawain commented.

"Here I am."

"Where've you been all day?"

"In the north woods, then on the high tower," Terence replied. Even to his own ears, his voice sounded abrupt. "Sorry, milord," he muttered.

"Still worried?" Gawain asked, turning to examine Terence more closely.

"Ay," Terence replied. "It's been nearly six months now since I've had any contact with the Other World."

Gawain shrugged. "Is that so rare? Until I began traveling with you — fifteen, twenty years ago, or whatever it was — I *never* had contact with the Other World."

"It's rare for me. Since we met, I've never gone more than a week or two without some word from home."

When Terence said *home* he always meant Avalon, the court of his father, Ganscotter, in the World of the Faeries. Terence had been raised as a foundling by a hermit until he had been taken on as squire many years before by the young Gawain. In the course of their adventures, Terence had discovered his faery heritage and, through many visits to the Other World since then, had come to realize that he lived in the World of Men as a visitor and a stranger.

Gawain nodded. Although he had only a trace of faery blood himself, he was as tied to Avalon in his own way as Terence was. In Avalon lived his wife, Lorie, who was Ganscotter's daughter and Terence's half sister. Both Terence and Gawain would have left the World of Men and returned to Avalon in a second if it were not for their loyalty to King Arthur. Ganscotter had told them that they still had a task to perform for their king, and so they remained — their lives and duty in one world, their hearts and hopes in another.

"What are you thinking?" asked Gawain. "Have you noticed something peculiar?"

Terence sighed and sat in the other armchair by the fire. It was a breach of courtly etiquette for a squire to sit in the presence of his knight, but they had been through far too much for either to give a straw for such rules. "No, nothing. I don't have one solid reason for feeling so uneasy. To all appearances, King Arthur's reign is at its peak. Everything is peaceful and prosperous. It's been more than a year since the last little revolt, and that was just poor, unhappy Count Anders being a silly ass. King Arthur's made England what every land ought to be, and people come from everywhere to see how he did it and to bask in his glory."

Gawain snorted and took a deep draught of ale. "I could do without that last bit," he commented, wiping foam from his lips with the back of his hand. "It's gotten so you can't step outside your door without tripping over another batch of jabbering, overdressed foreign courtiers come to get that Camelot polish, as if Arthur were running some sort of finishing school for knights. And that reminds me, where's this latest passel of fools from? The ones with the checkerboard trappings?"

A gruff voice came from the hallway behind Terence, through the still open door. "From the Holy Bleedin' Roman Empire." Neither Terence nor Gawain bothered to look. They both knew the voice of Sir Kai, King Arthur's half brother and seneschal.

"Come in, Kai," said Gawain. "Oh, you have. Have some . . . Never mind." Kai was already at the sideboard, helping himself to a tankard of ale.

He joined them by the fire and continued his own rumbling monologue. "Though why they call themselves Roman makes no manner of sense to me. A passel of Germans." He frowned. "Is that right? Is it a *passel* of Germans?"

Gawain looked thoughtful. "It isn't a *flock*, I know. Or a *gaggle*. For that matter, what would you call a group of Britons?"

Kai snorted. "All I know is that I wouldn't call them Roman."

Gawain assumed the patient tone of someone instructing a very small child, or an idiot, and said, "Let me explain then, my dear Kai. The founder of this empire was a very important man named Charlemagne, who was a very good Christian except for the bit about killing thousands of people, and so the pope himself granted him the title of Emperor of Rome. So now Charlemagne's successors are the spiritual descendants of the Roman Caesars."

"If there was anything spiritual about the Caesars I've yet to hear it," grunted Kai. "And anyway, it isn't as if the old Roman empire is gone. It's not what it once was, but it's still around, moved to Constantinople. So now, because the pope's a busybody without a lick of sense, we have *two* bleedin' Roman empires, and if I have to pick one I'll take the one that's farthest off. At least they're not sending us *their* wet-nosed brats to learn how to be knights."

Terence rose from his chair and slipped away. Kai and Gawain would be talking politics for hours, and he had no desire to listen. Outside the door, he took a long breath, then slipped out the window at the end of the corridor and climbed up the outside of the castle wall to a window one level up. He was going where he nearly always went when he felt uneasy or incomplete. He swung through the open window into a neat bedchamber where a red-haired woman sat reading. "Hello, love," Terence said.

Lady Eileen carefully marked her place in her book, then looked up and met Terence's smile. "Hello, Terence. I was hoping you'd come by today."

"Oh?" Terence asked. "Did you have something to ask me?"

"No," Eileen replied. "I hope that every day." She rose and walked across the room to him, and they kissed. It had been more than fifteen years since Terence and Gawain had rescued Lady Eileen from the Chateau Wirral, and Terence still caught his breath when he looked into her wise, laughing eyes. She rested her hands on Terence's shoulders, then stepped back to look at his face from arm's length. "Now you tell me," she said. "What's wrong?"

Terence shrugged. "It's the same thing. Still no contact from the Other World. Not even a visit from Robin." Robin was the name of a mischievous little sprite who had been Terence's most frequent faery visitor.

"And it worries you," Eileen said, nodding.

Terence nodded back. "Remember, when I was with my father six months ago, he told me there was a plot against Arthur and that I was to be on my guard. Since then, there's been no contact at all."

"You think this silence is a part of the plot?" Eileen asked. "That someone is keeping the two worlds apart on purpose? But who could do that?"

"Morgause," Terence replied at once. Morgause was

the most powerful, and most venomous, enchantress in Britain. She was also Gawain's mother and King Arthur's half sister, but that had no bearing on the implacable hatred that she bore for both. Terence and Gawain had opposed her plots against the king more than once.

"Remember a few years ago," Terence said, "when Morgause kidnapped Queen Guinevere? She took the queen to a deserted land and cast a spell over it that kept all faeries from entering. Even I couldn't go in, and I'm only half faery. Lancelot and Lady Sarah had to rescue the queen. What if Morgause has done something like that for all England?"

"I think you worry too much," Eileen said at last. "I'm no expert, but I have a feeling that if Morgause had enough power to do that, she wouldn't have to work by such roundabout means. She'd be able to just kill us all outright."

Terence relaxed. Of course Eileen was right. "That's why I keep coming to you. You have such good sense."

Eileen rolled her eyes. "Why, how complimentary, my dear! I had thought that you came because you were fond of me, but I see now that it's because I'm useful."

"Well, I wouldn't go that far," Terence replied, grinning. "But you show promise."

Eileen drew a breath to reply, but before she could speak, there came a loud rap on her chamber door and a thin female voice with a rich accent called out, "Lady Eileen! Are you een?"

"Oh, blast!" Eileen muttered.

"Who is it?"

"A little chit named Fenice," Eileen said in a low voice. "She's with this latest group of tourists from the Holy Roman Empire. A silly, pampered girl with a head full of nonsense about romance that she's picked up from bad minstrels. Quick, in my bedroom. I'll try to get rid of her, but she's not strong on taking hints."

Terence ducked behind Eileen's bedroom door. For Lady Eileen — one of Queen Guinevere's chief ladies-in-waiting — to be seen alone in her rooms with a lowly squire would effectively ruin her socially in the eyes of most of the court. He closed the door behind him and heard Eileen opening the outer door. "Good afternoon, Lady Fenice. What can I do for you?"

There was a swishing of silk, and Lady Fenice's voice grew clearer as she entered Eileen's sitting room. "Ah, my dear Lady Eileen, I haff just heard the saddest news! I am to return to my home and so must take my leave of you! And I haff been *so* happy here! And to think! I haff seen Sir Lancelot and Sir Gavain and Sir Yvain and so many of the greatest knights! It is, it is, *unglaubhaft* — I do not know the English word; wait, I haff it! It is *uncredible* to see in real life these heroes that one had only in legends thought to live! But you, you do not think so. These heroes are close to you all the time, is it not?"

"I have been here at Camelot many years," Eileen replied.

"But there is one you are perhaps closer to than others, yes?"

"I'm not sure I understand you, Lady Fenice."

"One you haff loved faithfully for many years. It is so, yes!"

Eileen hesitated, then replied, "I don't know to whom you've been talking, but I'm sure that whoever it was told you I have never been married."

"Married? But what has that to say to anything? I do not speak of marriage. I speak of love! Marriage is a contract, a . . . a *Notwendigkeit* . . . a thing that one cannot help. Me, I will be married soon, but it does not matter."

"You'll be married soon?"

"But yes. That is why my visit here must be cut short. A messenger comes to say that my father has arranged a marriage for me."

"A marriage to whom?"

"The Duke of Saxony. He's very rich and very old. He will do nicely. But I speak of *love!* I haff heard whispers of your secret love."

Terence leaned toward the door.

"You must learn not to pay attention to rumors, Lady Fenice," Eileen replied calmly.

"I haff been told how he rescued you from a castle called Wirr . . . called something silly and English, and how you have been faithful to him ever since, and how he has never married, for love of you! So I haff come to see you before I leave to hear stories of your love. How does he worship you? Does he poems of love to you write? Allegories? Does he wear your token at the tournaments? Do you send secret messages? Oh, it is so *wunderbar!* It is like Tristram and Iseult!"

"Sir Tristram and Lady Iseult had a disgraceful affair and both died because of it," Lady Eileen said abruptly.

"Yes," sighed Lady Fenice. "Isn't it *romantic?* But it isn't only Tristram and Iseult. I haff also heard that Queen Guinevere, many years ago —"

"I'm afraid I can't help you, Fenice," Eileen interrupted. "My congratulations on your upcoming marriage, and I wish you the very best of journeys as you return home."

Terence grinned and relaxed. He could just picture his Eileen shepherding the Lady Fenice gently but irresistibly out the door. Taking a breath, he stepped back, bumped against a chest, and knocked a wooden basin onto the stone floor. It made an impressive clatter as it bounced.

"Aha! I *knew* it!" shrieked a delighted voice, and a

moment later the bedroom door had been thrown open and Terence looked into the eyes of a pretty yellow-haired girl in a sumptuous silk dress. "I was right!" she exclaimed. "Secret messages!"

Terence avoided Eileen's eyes and cast about desperately for something to say. Nothing came to him.

"He sends his *squire* to you with love messages!" Fenice said. "Me, I haff seen this squire, and I know!" She turned back to Eileen and said, "You and Sir Gavain are very sly, yes? But you may trust me! I will say nothing! Oh, it is so *romantic!*"

With that, Lady Fenice swished away. Eileen looked steadily at Terence for a long second. "Oh, marvelous. Terence, the uncanny woodsman who can creep through the densest of shrubbery without a sound! Can't make it across a blinking bedroom, can you?"

"I am, er, better in the woods," Terence admitted.

"And now she's off telling everyone about my love for Gawain."

"She said she would tell no one," Terence pointed out.

Eileen shook her head sadly. "You weren't listening. What she really said was 'I can't wait to tell everyone I meet.'"

"*That's* what she said?"

"Of course. Soon the whole court will think I've had a long-standing affair with Gawain."

"Well, at least you both have good taste," Terence said.

"Shut up, my love."

That evening King Arthur was hosting a state dinner for his guests from the Holy Roman Empire. In recent years, state dinners had become the most frequent event at court. When alone in Gawain's chambers, with those he trusted, Sir Kai would often complain about such affairs. "When I started out," he would say, "I organized armies and planned for battles. Now I spend my time making sure that the linens are clean for the banquet tables." And if anyone suggested to him that it was the price of peace, Sir Kai would reply, "Not sure it's worth it."

Having no plausible excuse to skip the banquet, Gawain went, which meant that Terence was there as well, standing correctly behind his knight's chair. He didn't mind. He, at least, could move about the room and stretch his legs. This evening, as dinner entertainment, the guests from the continent offered their very own minstrel — a spindly fellow named Gottfried — to sing a song of his own composition. After apologizing to all for his English, which actually was excellent, the minstrel launched into the tale of Sir Tristram de Liones and his adulterous love affair with Queen Iseult, wife of King Mark of Cornwall. Gottfried played it up in the best courtly tradition, praising the purity of the pair's love and treating King Mark as a jealous buffoon. Never once did he hint that King Mark might have had reason to be angry about his wife's love affair with another. Terence decided that this would be a good time to stretch his legs, and he casually made his way to the kitchens.

He had been there only a few seconds when the doors opened again and he was joined by one of King Arthur's knights, Sir Dinadan. "Is the dinner over?" asked Terence, grinning.

Sir Dinadan smiled back, ruefully. "I couldn't stomach it," he admitted. "Even leaving aside that this Gottfried has no touch for his instrument — he plays the lyre like he's currying a horse — I just can't sit still and hear Tristram and Iseult treated as tragic heroes instead of the selfish lackwits that they really were."

Terence's eyes rested on Dinadan's face. "Don't I remember hearing . . . you were there, weren't you?"

Dinadan nodded. "I saw them die, and there was nothing noble or romantic about it. It was stupid and pointless." Dinadan made a quick head motion as if to shake off a fly, then crossed through the kitchen and went out the far door. Terence watched him thoughtfully. When Dinadan had first arrived at Camelot, a callow youth not knowing whether he wanted to be a knight or a minstrel, Terence had not thought much of him, but in late years he had reconsidered that opinion. At any rate, he felt a bond of sympathy with anyone who lived in one world but really belonged in another.

Gottried finished his maudlin poem, to loud cheers from the younger knights and courtiers and polite applause from the older ones, and Terence returned to his place behind Gawain, who whispered to him, "Coward!" Terence grinned but didn't answer.

As the third course was concluding, a diversion broke the predictable monotony of the state dinner. A guard hurried into the hall, spoke privately with King Arthur for several seconds, then trotted away. After a moment, Arthur and Queen Guinevere rose to their feet. "My friends, I apologize for the interruption, but we have just received word that a dear friend has arrived at the court, and we must leave you for a moment." He smiled to the party from the Holy Roman Empire and said, "We shall not be gone long. Indeed, I hope to persuade our guest to join our dinner."

A buzz of whispers began as soon as King Arthur and Queen Guinevere were gone. Terence exchanged a glance with Gawain, but neither joined in the speculation. They would be told who this guest was when the king was ready. Sure enough, a minute later, the king and queen returned, with their guest between them. She was a young lady with reddish-blond hair and a firm step. Terence smiled with genuine pleasure.

"My lords and ladies," King Arthur announced. "I present to you the Lady Sarah of Milrick."

The king needed to say no more. Everyone at Camelot — and, from their awed expressions, even those from the Holy Roman Empire — had heard of Lady Sarah. Only a few years had passed since she, aided by Sir Lancelot, had rescued Queen Guinevere from a knight who had kidnapped her, a certain Sir Meliagant. Since then, Lady Sarah had lived quietly in the small castle that King Arthur had given her and had not been to Camelot, but Terence and Gawain had ridden with her for a time on that adventure and knew her very well. From the king's table, Sir Lancelot rose to his feet and crossed the hall to Lady Sarah. "My lady," he said reverently, kneeling at her feet.

Lady Sarah suppressed a smile. "Oh, get up, Lancelot. It's good to see you again, too." She stood in the center of the hall, clad in her dusty traveling clothes, and gazed around the brilliantly decorated room filled with richly clothed courtiers and foreign dignitaries. "Forgive me for interrupting your dinner," she said, "but I *am* hungry." Queen Guinevere took her arm and began leading her to the head table, but as they passed by Sir Gawain's seat, Lady Sarah looked intently into Terence's eyes and mouthed the words, "Can we talk?"

Until the contingent from the Holy Roman Empire left, there were no available guest rooms at Camelot, which Terence used to his advantage. By strolling among the tables during the dinner, dropping a word in Kai's ear and whispering for a moment with Eileen, he saw to it that Sarah was assigned to stay with Eileen during her time at Camelot. Having arranged that, it was easy for him simply to drop in on Eileen after dinner, once he was sure that Sarah was there. Sarah and Eileen were sitting by the fire when he swung through the open window, and Sarah gave a start. "Lud!" she exclaimed. "Does he often do that?"

"No manners at all," Eileen said without looking up from her embroidery.

Sarah glanced curiously at Eileen, then at Terence. Terence said, "It's good to see you again, my lady. You're looking well. Older, but well."

"And you look exactly the same," Sarah said frankly.

"He never ages," Eileen commented, setting a tiny stitch. "It's infuriating."

"And how about our mutual friends? Lady Charis?" Terence went on. "I trust she's well? And Ariel?"

Sarah frowned. "Charis is fine," she said. "I haven't seen Ariel in months."

Terence allowed nothing to show, but his heart sank. Ariel was from the World of Faeries.

"That's what brought me here," Sarah continued. "Ariel used to drop in every week or two, and then about six months ago, her visits stopped." Eileen looked up from her stitching, met Terence's eyes, then looked down again. Sarah went on, "I was concerned, but I didn't want to overreact and get all worried over nothing."

"I know just what you mean," Terence said.

"Then someone came to me and gave me a message for you."

"Someone?"

Sarah hesitated, glancing quickly at Eileen. "I was told to tell no one but you," she said.

"Who told you that?"

Sarah considered this. "Well, she didn't say I wasn't to identify *her*. It was Lady Morgan."

Terence nodded. Morgan Le Fay was another of Gawain's aunts, an enchantress like her malevolent sister Morgause, but not as dependably wicked. "I see," Terence said. "Well, you can take my word for it that you may trust Eileen."

"Still . . ." Sarah said.

"If it makes any difference, let me assure you that whatever you tell me in private, I will certainly tell Eileen. So why not save time and tell us both?"

Sarah looked between the two one more time, a faint smile on her lips, then shrugged. "All right. She said to tell you that it has started again, and that this time there would be no help from your world."

She paused, and Terence asked, "Is that it?"

"No, but what does that much mean?"

"It means," Terence said, "that Morgause the Enchantress has begun yet another plot to destroy Arthur."

"That's what I thought. She was the one behind the queen's abduction, wasn't she? And when she says there will be no help from your world, that means the faery world, doesn't it?" Terence nodded. "Why not?"

"I haven't any idea."

Sarah frowned. "How disappointing," she said. "I had come to think that you knew everything."

"A lot of people think that," Eileen said. "Odd, isn't it?"

"What else did Morgan tell you?"

"She said that this time the threat would come through pretense and falsehood. And that's it. Oh, except that she said that you're to trust no one."

Terence nodded. "Yes," he said. "Morgan isn't very trustworthy herself, so she has trouble understanding the concept of trust. But I don't choose to live like that." He pursed his lips and thought for a moment. "Well, that doesn't help much, but at least it confirms what I've been feeling. Thank you, Sarah."

He fell again into a reverie, so that he was only vaguely aware of Eileen asking calmly, "Do you make a long stay at Camelot, Sarah?"

"I should like to stay for a while, anyway," Sarah replied, "but I don't want to put you out."

"Oh, it's no trouble. My rooms are quite large enough for two people."

20

Sarah looked puzzled. "Two people? You mean you usually live here alone?"

"Yes," Eileen replied. "Had you heard otherwise?"

"No, but . . ."

"But what?"

Sarah took a breath. "I'm probably breaking some important rule of courtly etiquette that I never learned correctly, but I never understood why it's sometimes ill manners to say out loud what's obvious." She looked at Eileen, then at Terence, then back at Eileen. "I assumed that you two were married."

Terence and Eileen both stared at her, but neither spoke.

"It's as plain as day. I've never seen two people who fit together as perfectly and who were as comfortable with each other as you two are. You love each other. If you aren't married, then it's a crying shame. Are you?"

"Yes," Terence said.

"In a manner of speaking," added Eileen. "Mostly."

"What does that mean?" demanded Sarah. "I didn't think you could be *mostly* married."

Terence hesitated, not really wanting to tell Sarah what was known only to the two of them and Gawain, but he had every reason to trust Sarah. Besides, he had just declared in front of her that he refused to be as untrusting as Morgan, so he said, "About fifteen years ago —"

"Sixteen," corrected Eileen, who had gone back to her embroidery.

"Sixteen, then. Eileen and I had a private sort of wedding ceremony. It was just a few months after Gawain and I brought her to court. We slipped out on our own and went to a religious man that I knew, named Trevisant, and with him as a witness we promised to love each other faithfully."

"Then you're married," Sarah said.

"Sort of," Eileen said.

"It's not exactly official," Terence admitted.

"Why not?"

"Well, Trevisant was a holy man, as I said, but he wasn't a priest."

"Oh." Sarah seemed to digest this for a moment. "So why not go to a real priest? Why the secrecy?"

"We went to Trevisant because he was the man who raised me," Terence said. Then he grinned ruefully. "Also because I knew that he would forget it within a few days. Trevisant was peculiar that way. You see, I'm a squire — and as far as the court is aware, a squire of unknown parentage. Lady Eileen is a noblewoman from one of the oldest families in England. For her to marry so far beneath herself would ruin her socially."

Sarah glanced at Eileen. "Does that matter to you?"

Eileen smiled briefly. "At the time it did, a little. At any rate, I agreed to the plan readily enough. It doesn't seem so important anymore, but it still matters to Terence."

"And so," Sarah said, "for fifteen years —"

"Sixteen," said Eileen.

"Sixteen, I mean. For sixteen years, you've been married, sort of, mostly, but have told no one."

"Gawain knows," Terence said. "But, yes, that's essentially it."

"Haven't you ever thought about going ahead and making it official?"

This time Eileen replied. "Yes, of course we have. But the longer the current arrangement goes on, the harder that becomes. To get married now, suddenly, after years of pretending to be only casual friends, would give rise to all sorts of speculation as to what had really been going on all that time. And if we explained that we hadn't been having an affair, that we had really been married —"

"Mostly," Terence qualified.

"Sort of," added Sarah.

Eileen ignored them. "As I say, if we told people we'd been married all along, then we would have to explain why we'd deceived them. Awkward."

"And besides," Terence said, "we are, as you say, comfortable together. There hasn't really seemed to be a need to change."

Sarah looked dubious, but Terence reminded himself that she was still young. Young people sometimes place excessive value on external forms and ceremonies, he remembered, so he let it go.

"And now, Terence," Eileen said, breaking into his thoughts, "you go report to Gawain and Arthur and whoever you feel should know Sarah's news. We ladies will go to bed. It really isn't seemly for a man to be in our quarters so late, you know. We're virtuous ladies, we are."

"Virtuous?" repeated Terence.

"Sort of," said Eileen.

"Mostly," added Sarah.

2

ALEXANDER OF CONSTANTINOPLE

Terence stood beside Kai and watched the last courtier from the Holy Roman Empire ride out the castle gates. It was shortly after noon the day after the state dinner, and Kai had worked tirelessly all morning to see that nothing prevented their leaving. Kai was always competent, but when he was speeding the departure of a large party of visiting dignitaries, he was brilliantly efficient. "Close the gates!" he called to the guards.

"Close the gates?" repeated the guard captain. "But it's midday. The standing orders —"

"I don't care what the standing orders are!" snapped Kai. "We just got rid of that lot. If we leave the gates open, someone else'll come in." The captain grinned and did nothing. He had known Kai a long time and was familiar with his moods. After a moment, Kai shrugged and said, "Oh, all right. Suit yourself, Alan.

Stick to your orders if you have to, but don't blame me if the next batch is even worse."

For his part, Terence was as glad to see the Germans leave as Kai was, though for different reasons. Morgan's warning the night before had put him on his guard. Nothing Morgan could say would make him distrust his friends, but he didn't mind seeing some of the strangers at Camelot leave.

A trumpet blared from the tallest watchtower, and a shout drifted down. "Party coming from the east! It's a big one!"

Kai's jaw dropped, and for a second he was speechless. Then, for several more seconds, he uttered a series of short, very blunt words. Terence sympathized with him. He didn't use those particular words himself, but he had to admit that sometimes they felt right. "Want me to go tell Arthur?" he asked.

"See who it is first," grumbled Kai. "Maybe somebody just passing through."

Another shout came from the tower. "Advance party approaching!"

Terence walked with Kai to the main gate and waited. A minute later they perceived two horsemen approaching at a gallop, and as they drew near Terence saw that they were dressed in sumptuous silks and mounted on magnificent horses. These were no mere passersby. Kai sighed. The two riders dismounted at the gate. One was a lean, middle-aged man with a neat beard, and the other was a smiling youth. Both bowed to Kai, and the older man said in perfect but accented English, "I bid you good day, sir. Am I correct that this is Camelot, the seat of King Arthur Pendragon?"

"It is," Kai replied.

"And is the king residing here at present?"

The man's manners were a perfect blend of deference and dignity. Kai appeared to thaw slightly. "Forgive me, but may I know who is asking?"

The older man inclined his head graciously. "Of course. I am Acoriondes of Athens, and this boy is my squire, Bernard. We come in company with my master, the Emperor of Rome."

Terence blinked, and even Kai looked startled. "Who? Do you mean the Holy Roman Emperor?"

Acoriondes smiled. "Do you speak of the new empire that claims the heritage of Rome? No, we come from the original empire, from Constantinople. My master is Emperor Alexander. Having heard of King Arthur's glory and wisdom, we have traveled from our distant home to meet him and learn from him."

Terence cleared his throat. "*Now* should I go get the king?"

Kai nodded gravely. "Ay, Terence. Now you can do that."

Twenty minutes later, King Arthur and most of the knights and ladies of the court were gathered in the main yard to welcome their distinguished guests. Over the past years, some of the greatest rulers of Europe had visited Camelot, but none of such power and influence as the Emperor of Rome. It was true, as Kai had said the day before, that the current empire had lost much of its former power in the past few centuries. The empire of the Caesars had included most of Europe and the entire northern coast of Africa, but since that day the nations of western Europe had broken away and Africa had been conquered by the people of Mohammed. Still, though, from its capital at Constantinople, the empire covered lands many times the size of Britain. For the Emperor of Rome to visit Arthur was a great honor.

Since the messenger, Acoriondes, had announced the emperor, the imperial party had had plenty of time to arrive, but they seemed to be in no hurry, doubtless to give the English time to prepare a suitable welcome. At last, though, the party arrived, led by a black-bearded knight in flashing silver armor. The silver knight came to a halt and gazed around the castle courtyard with undisguised excitement. Then his eyes rested on King Arthur, who was sitting on a velvet-covered throne in the center of the courtyard, and the knight nearly threw himself from his horse.

"You are King Arthur!" the knight called in English. It wasn't a question. "No! Do not say! I see for my own eyes! You are wisdom and greatness!" He rushed forward and threw himself at King Arthur's feet. "I am Alexander, emperor at Constantinopolis, but I am your servant!"

King Arthur blinked with surprise. Alexander bent his head as if to kiss the king's feet, but Arthur caught his shoulder. "Nay, Your Highness!" Arthur said quickly. "You owe me no such obeisance! Stand, I beg you."

Terence had watched this scene with only half his attention. With one eye he had been watching the courtier, Acoriondes, who had arrived immediately behind Emperor Alexander. When his master had prostrated himself before Arthur, Acoriondes had frowned, very slightly, but at Arthur's swift response, he relaxed. He nodded and gave the king a look of approval.

King Arthur continued, "You are the Emperor of Rome?"

Alexander smiled brightly. "It is what I am told to say. But it is silly, no? My capital is Constantinopolis. In the city called Rome, I have no power at all. There it is your pope who rules. But my counselors all tell me I must pretend to be Caesar Augustus, and so I say, 'Yes, I am the Emperor of Rome.'"

Acoriondes looked pained again, but Arthur chuckled at his noble guest's frankness. "And I, for my part," he said, "am supposed to call myself Arthur Pendragon, King of All England, Duke of Brittany, and several other things that I don't recall at the moment. It is, as you say, rather silly. If we have to speak of each other this way, we shall never be able to hold a conversation. Shall we break all the rules of diplomacy, you and I? I wish you would simply call me Arthur."

Alexander's eyes shone. "And you must call me Alexander!"

"Then I welcome you, Alexander, to my court. You do me great honor with your visit. Allow me to present to you my friend and seneschal, Sir Kai. If you or any of your court needs anything at all, you must speak to Kai."

"I have heard of you, Sir Kai! In the songs, they call you Kai, the Slayer of Kings!"

Nothing irritated Kai more than enthusiasm, but with an effort he managed to say only, "Honored, Your Highness."

Alexander turned and gestured to his retinue. "You put my mind on my manners, Arthur. I must introduce you Acoriondes, the empire's first counselor. He should have stayed with my uncle, but he comes with me to keep me from . . . what is the English saying, Acoriondes?"

"Embarrassing yourself, Your Highness?" Acoriondes said drily.

"Yes, of course! It is a heavy task, no? Also, Acoriondes speaks your language well! So I could not spare him for my uncle."

"Your uncle?" inquired Arthur.

"My father's brother. I left him as regent over the empire while I am away. He did not wish it, but he agreed. Dear Uncle Alis!"

Kai coughed slightly. "Your uncle is named Alice?"

"Yes. Is it not a name found in England?"

"Well, it is," Kai admitted. "I myself know several Alices, but —"

Acoriondes cleared his throat. "It is a Greek name," he explained. "In your letters it would be spelled A-L-I-S."

Alexander laughed. "But you are like a schoolteacher, Acoriondes! No one cares how it is spelled!"

"I thought it might explain things, Your Highness," Acoriondes said with a slight bow.

"And there, on the white horse, is my young brother, Cligés."

The young man that Alexander had indicated smiled eagerly and leaped from his horse to bow before King Arthur. "I am . . . happy to m-meeting you," he stammered. "And please, is Sir Lancelot here?"

The counselor, Acoriondes, gave Cligés a stern look, which the youth ignored, but King Arthur only smiled. He was accustomed to young knights who had little interest in a mere king when they could be admiring his most famous champion.

"Of course," the king said, indicating Lancelot at his left. "Sir Lancelot, allow me to introduce you to Prince Cligés."

Cligés blinked at Lancelot with obvious surprise. Among the brightly clad courtiers who filled the court, Lancelot's simple clothes seemed almost shabby. Lancelot bowed gracefully. "It is an honor, O prince," he said. "But your name, Cligés — is it not French?"

The prince nodded vehemently. "Yes! My Greek name is like it, but, *moi, j'aime mieux* the French. You are from childhood my hero, Sir Lancelot!" Then he knelt at Lancelot's feet.

Acoriondes looked pained again: Cligés had shown greater reverence for the knight than for the king. But Alexander only grinned. "Cligés loves all things French. Indeed, we passed two weeks with the Count of Champagne on our way here, and we would still be there if Cligés could choose." He waved his arm at the rest of his retinue. "As for the rest, you will never remember all their names. Some are knights, and the rest are servants, which I bring to make our visit easy for you."

Kai looked sourly at Alexander's huge retinue, more than a hundred and fifty persons in all, including at least twenty mounted knights and a dozen wagons. "Oh, ay, easy," he muttered. "The thing is, Your Majesty, we may not have enough guest rooms for all —"

Alexander snapped his fingers. "I see there is a town outside the castle walls. Has it a . . . a . . ." He glanced at Acoriondes. "A *pandocheion*?"

"An inn, Your Highness."

Arthur blinked. "Yes, of course. There are several inns there, but I could not permit —"

"Good! I will buy two of them!" Alexander declared. "I bring my own furnishes so to do this! Acoriondes, see to it!"

The grave courtier bowed, but before starting away he addressed King Arthur again. "Your Highness," he said, "I do not think you will change my master's mind in this. We are your guests, of course, and we will accept with gratitude what hospitality you offer. But it is not our intention to make ourselves unwelcome. We have brought all that we require to set up our own household outside your walls."

Arthur pursed his lips, but evidently decided that it was best to submit with good grace. "Then you must allow me to host you and your knights at a dinner this very evening. Kai?"

Kai nodded resignedly. "A state dinner. Naturally."

Arthur's eyes wrinkled with amusement, and he added, "And perhaps in two days, a tournament in honor of our noble guests?"

"A tournament, too," Kai repeated bleakly. "It needed but that."

"Yes, that's what I thought," Arthur said, smiling impishly at his friend.

"A tournament! I have heard of your tournaments!" exclaimed Alexander. Cligés looked so excited that Terence thought he might pass out.

"Your Highness?" Terence said.

"Yes, Terence?"

"Perhaps I could accompany Sir Acoriondes and help him find suitable quarters in the town." Arthur nodded, and Terence turned to the tall dignitary. "I am Squire Terence, and I will be honored to serve you. Will you follow me, please?"

It took no time at all to make the necessary arrangements. Terence led the imperial party to the main thoroughfare in the town, where two large stone inns stood beside each other, and Acoriondes nodded his approval. Terence hadn't been sure the innkeepers would be willing to sell their inns outright, but when Acoriondes dropped a huge bag of gold at each man's feet, as carelessly as if he were tossing seed to chickens, both agreed at once. Then the army of servants that Alexander had brought with him set about turning the inns into a suitable residence for their emperor. All the rough, sturdy English furniture was tossed into the streets and replaced with the finest of upholstered chairs and grand gilded beds and sumptuous carpets and embroidered drapes. The whole town gathered to gawk as the imperial wagons were unloaded, but Terence only watched until Acoriondes finished giving instructions and started back toward the castle gates on foot.

Terence fell into step beside him but said nothing. Acoriondes had been aloof toward him, and Terence guessed that it was because he was a lowly squire. Neither spoke until they were back in the now empty main courtyard. Then Acoriondes turned to Terence. "Please, Squire Terence," he said austerely. "I would be grateful if you could tell me where I could find my master now?"

Terence didn't have to answer. At that moment Acoriondes's own squire, the youth Bernard, came dashing from the central keep of the castle, calling out something to Acoriondes in agitated tones. Acoriondes closed his eyes wearily, asked several sharp questions, then followed Bernard back inside with a firm step. Bemused, Terence watched them go. After a moment he noticed Eileen approaching.

"Did you see that?" Terence asked. Eileen nodded. "I wonder what's gotten that young fellow in such a stew."

"Well," Eileen said, "I can't say for sure, since I don't speak Greek."

"Is that what they speak? I wondered."

"But if I had to guess," Eileen continued calmly, "I

would say he was telling his master that Alexander, Emperor of Constantinople, has just asked Sarah to marry him."

"What am I supposed to do?" Sarah demanded in exasperation. It was just before the state dinner for the visitors from Constantinople. Terence and Gawain had stopped by Eileen's chambers to escort her and Sarah.

"By what Guinevere told me," Eileen said, "you handled it very well."

"I put him off for a while," Sarah said. "That's all."

"What actually happened?" asked Gawain. "I've heard three different stories already, and none of them make sense."

"It *doesn't* make sense!" Sarah said. "It was right after the little welcome ceremony in the courtyard. I'd gone off with Guinevere to her rooms, just to catch up, and a moment later King Arthur showed up with this Alexander. He wanted to introduce him to the queen, I suppose, but naturally he introduced us both. So then Alexander fawned over us both for a minute, telling us how beautiful we both are and rot like that, and then, out of the blue, he dropped on one knee and asked if I would be his empress."

"What did you say?" Gawain asked, his eyes bright.

"I said I'd just met him and that I could hardly

marry a complete stranger. So he smiled and said he looked forward to getting to know me better."

"How . . . romantic," said Gawain unsteadily. He was trying to conceal his amusement, but he wasn't very good at it.

"That's what Guinevere said," snorted Sarah. "She says it's the most beautiful thing she's ever heard, just like in the minstrel's love songs. And it *is,* too! It's *exactly* like that rubbish. What in the world would possess a man to propose to someone he met twenty seconds before?"

"Does the emperor know anything about you?" asked Terence suddenly.

"Obviously not," replied Gawain. "He proposed to her, didn't he?"

"Shut up, Gawain," Sarah replied absently. "No, nothing really. Arthur just introduced me as his cousin Lady Sarah." She frowned. "Surely that's not it. Just wanting to marry into Arthur's family?"

"I've no idea," Terence admitted. "I was just wondering."

"Well, while you're wondering, why don't you wonder how I'm going to avoid this Alexander? Should I skip the dinner tonight?"

"Afraid?" asked Gawain.

"Yes."

Gawain shook his head slowly. "Lancelot tells me

how you once faced a fully armored knight in single combat," he pointed out.

"Kid stuff," Sarah replied.

Eileen, who had been waiting patiently by the door through all this, finally spoke. "Sarah, don't be foolish. You're making a great deal out of nothing. You will come to dinner tonight and will be polite to the emperor. If he asks you again to marry him, you will answer. If you don't care for the idea, you will say no. Now come along. We're going to be late."

Sarah and Gawain and Terence murmured, "Yes, ma'am," and followed.

Though he watched Emperor Alexander closely during the dinner, Terence still could not tell what had prompted his marriage proposal. That he regarded King Arthur with great reverence was obvious, so it was possible that he had asked Sarah to marry him so as to form an alliance with his hero. On the other hand, his expression when he looked at Sarah was undeniably filled with admiration. Sarah, for her part, was quellingly polite, replying to all Alexander's comments tersely and with a cold correctness. No matter how earnestly the emperor begged her to call him Alexander, she continued to refer to him as *Your Highness*. But Alexander didn't seem at all discouraged.

"Dearest Lady Sarah," Alexander said during the

third course, "it is your maidenly reserve that is most admirable. I do not know anyone like you."

Gawain's shoulders shook convulsively, and Terence guessed that his friend was remembering how Sarah had once beheaded an attacking knight. In a colorless voice, Sarah replied, "It is kind of you to say so, Your Highness."

"My lord," said Acoriondes, "look at that coat of arms opposite you, with the twin lions. Is that not like the crest that you admired at Lady Maximilla's palace in Macedonia?"

"Yes. I don't know. Perhaps," Alexander replied without looking. "It is of no importance. Lady Sarah, I should like to show you the Aegean Sea. It is the bluest of seas, yet it is nothing before your eyes."

"My eyes are green, Your Highness."

"And yet to me they are the purest of opal, and more precious."

"Emperor Alexander," said Guinevere, "tell Sarah what you were telling me earlier, about your castle in Athens."

"My court is at Constantinopolis," Alexander began, "but my fathers came from Macedon and Achaia — in Greece — and so I have a summer palace at Athens, of pure white marble, like the pure white of your . . ." He hesitated, then asked Acoriondes a question in Greek.

"Like the pure the white of your cheek," Acoriondes interpreted.

"No, no, that is not what I meant," Alexander protested. "I know *cheek.*"

"It had better be what you meant, my lord," Acoriondes said woodenly. "My lord, I wonder which armor you shall choose to wear at the tournament in two days' time."

"Ah, the tournament!" exclaimed Alexander. "It is in the songs of the troubadors that a knight must wear on his armor the . . . I-do-not-know-the-word of his lady, is it not so?"

"*Token,* Your Highness," Queen Guinevere supplied. "And, yes, it is often done so. A lady will give her knight a sleeve or a shawl to wear as a token in the jousting."

"My lady Sarah, I beg you to give me your sleeve!" Alexander cried.

"I am sorry to disappoint you, Your Highness, but I have need of all my sleeves."

"You could give him a shawl," Guinevere suggested. "One of your lovely embroidered ones." She turned to Alexander and explained, "Sarah does the most beautiful needlework!"

"She is a model woman, yes? To be so beautiful and also so talented!" Alexander replied.

"It's because I was raised by a Jewish textile merchant," Sarah said bluntly.

Alexander burst into laughter and renewed his entreaties for a scrap of cloth, but Sarah refused again.

Then young Cligés, seated at Alexander's side, spoke up. "You must not press her, my brother. It would not be *à la courtoise*. She should give you the token secretly, and then all the court would try to guess whose token you wear. And your love must not be easy. You must suffer first."

"I must suffer?" Alexander asked blankly. "Why?"

"It is how it is done, my brother," Cligés explained firmly. "*Si la dard est entrée par l'œil, pourquoi souffre le cœur dans la poitrine?*"

Terence spoke some French, but didn't catch this. Now a new voice joined the conversation. This was Sir Dinadan, seated at a nearby table. "O Emperor Alexander, didn't I hear you say you spent some time in Champagne?"

"Yes, for many days we were there."

"I thought I recognized that line," Dinadan commented.

"You know the French song I was quoting?" Cligés asked, delighted. "Is it not of the finest?"

Dinadan nodded agreeably. "Yes, indeed it is not," he replied.

"That was from a song?" asked Guinevere. "What does it mean?"

"*'If love enters through the eye, why does the heart suffer in the breast?'*" Dinadan translated. Then he

41

gave Acoriondes an impish glance and said, "Or should I say *cheek?*"

The statesman said nothing. Cligés ignored them both, still looking earnestly at his brother. "Yes, that is what I mean. If you love, you must suffer first in the heart!"

Sarah pushed her chair back from the table and rose. "I quite understand; I have a touch of indigestion myself." She turned to Arthur. "O king, forgive me, but I should like to lie down."

"Of course," the king said, sympathy in his voice. "Alexander and Acoriondes, I wonder if you could tell me more about the empire. I suppose, since you have traveled so far, that you are at peace now?"

For the rest of the evening, Arthur and Acoriondes talked about treaties and boundary disputes and the difficulties of governing distant territories. Alexander added little to this conversation. He looked disappointed and glanced often at the door through which Sarah had disappeared, to the interest and excitement of nearly everyone at dinner — especially Cligés.

The first day of the tournament arrived, and it was all Terence and Eileen could do to get Sarah to attend the event. For a whole day Sarah had managed to avoid Alexander, and she didn't want to ruin it now. But when Eileen pointed out that since everyone else would be at the tournament, staying behind would make it easy for someone to find her alone, Sarah grudgingly agreed to go, on the condition that no one would touch any of her sleeves.

Once there, it seemed as if Sarah had been worrying about nothing, because there was no Alexander to be found. Cligés and several of the Greek knights did well in the individual jousting, but Alexander did not appear. Just before the lists were closed, though, an unknown knight in black armor appeared from nowhere. He did not speak, but with gestures indicated his wish to compete. Arthur waved his permission.

"Golly," said Kai, seated beside Arthur in the stands. "I wonder who *this* could be."

Terence grinned and strolled away, finding himself before long standing near Dinadan, who never competed in tournaments. Dinadan met Terence's eye and grinned. "A mystery knight in black armor," he said with an expressive sigh. "And if he wins, what do you want to bet that he gives the prize to Lady Sarah?"

"It's hard to imagine who he thinks he's fooling," Terence admitted.

"It's not about fooling people," Dinadan said. "It's about playing the part."

"What part do you mean?" Terence asked.

"Remember that French love song that young Cligés was quoting the other night?" Dinadan asked.

Terence nodded. "Well, it's one of a new sort of knightly song they're singing on the continent — not about adventures but courtly love."

"What do you mean, 'courtly love'?" Terence asked. "Is that a special sort?"

"Lord, yes," Dinadan said. "Courtly lovers are all the most frightful asses."

"Nothing special about that," Terence pointed out. "I'd think that was normal for lovers."

"But *courtly* lovers," Dinadan explained loftily, "are noble and tragic asses. Usually there's a knight who's desperately stuck on some other man's wife —"

"Ah, I see," Terence interrupted. "That German minstrel's song about Tristram and Iseult the other evening."

"One of their favorite tales," Dinadan agreed. "And one thing the courtly lover does in just about every tale is dress up in someone else's armor, so as to win a tournament for his beloved without betraying their secret love."

"Ah," Terence said.

"Ah indeed," replied Dinadan, nodding. "If, as he said, Alexander spent weeks in Champagne listening to this nonsense, then he has some very odd ideas about how things are done at court." Dinadan gave Terence a measured look, then added, "You might mention this to Sarah, in fact, because if she's really not interested in Alexander, she's doing the wrong thing."

"What do you mean?"

"In courtly love, the lady is *supposed* to act disdainful and to heap scorn on her lover in public. It's part of the game. Plus it gives him a chance to be abused by her, which is seen as a good thing."

"Why, for heaven's sake?"

"Don't ask me. I don't sing this trash. But whatever the reason, there it is. The lady nearly always treats the knight like a dog that's been rolling in something smelly."

"So what should Sarah do instead?"

Dinadan pursed his lips thoughtfully. "She might leave the country," he suggested.

Terence sighed. "I'll tell her," he said as he walked on. Behind him he heard the clash of arms, but he couldn't muster any interest in whether Alexander had just won his first joust, so he kept walking. As he left the tournament encampment in the fields west of the city, he saw a knight riding toward him from the castle. Terence didn't recognize the armor, and when the knight drew close, he saw that he didn't recognize the knight's face either.

"May I help you?" Terence asked.

The knight, a young man with fair hair, smiled at him. "I hope so, O squire. I am looking for King

Arthur. At the castle they told me he was at this tournament."

"Are you a messenger?"

"Nothing so important, I'm afraid," the knight said. A strange chill began to creep over Terence, like nothing he had ever felt. He glanced about but saw nothing threatening. Then he looked back at the young knight with the ready smile, who said, "I'm just a wandering knight who thought I might try whether King Arthur would have me at his court."

"I'll take you to him," Terence offered. "What may I say your name is?"

"I'm called Mordred."

3

The Secret Prince

Terence heard the sound of children's shouts at least five minutes before he rode out of the trees and saw the hermitage. Reining in his horse at the edge of the yard, he surveyed the scene before him. He had known many holy retreats before — indeed, he had been raised in one — but he had never seen one quite so busy or noisy. At the far side of the clearing, near a bubbling spring, six or seven children were alternately working and arguing as they constructed a play fort of fallen branches. Beside the tiny hut, two older children, one boy and one girl, worked with axes, cutting wood for the woodpile. Another group of children, of varying ages, sat in the bare yard, writing letters and pronouncing them aloud while a girl of about fifteen watched and listened. And on a wooden stool in a sunny spot by the front door, clad in the full brown robe of a religious man, sat the hermit himself, looking hardly older than the youths around him.

Terence grinned and dismounted. "Hello, Brother Guinglain," he said.

The hermit rose to his feet and returned the smile. "Hello, Terence. I'm very glad to see you."

Terence raised one eyebrow. Despite Guinglain's relative youth, Terence had great faith in his discernment. It occurred to him that if anyone had news from the Other World, it might be Guinglain. "That sounds as if you had a particular reason for wanting to see me," he ventured.

"Oh, no," Guinglain replied, still smiling. "I'm very glad to see everyone."

Terence had to chuckle. Six months before, he and Gawain had traveled for several weeks with Guinglain, but Terence still found the young man somehow disconcerting. It wasn't that he was different from what he appeared to be; it was rather that he was exactly what he seemed. Terence wasn't sure he had ever met a human like him. "That would explain the crowd," Terence commented.

"Yes," Guinglain replied simply. "Sunday afternoons are like this. Many parents in the village let their children visit me after mass. Part of their religious education, I think."

An especially vehement dispute broke out near the play fort as two boys argued over the placement of a log. "I see," Terence said drily. "And those boys are learning their catechism, I suppose?"

"No," Guinglain said. "At the moment they're learning justice and respect for others. How have you been? How is Gawain? And King Arthur?"

"We are all well, and the kingdom is at peace, at least to all appearances."

Guinglain said nothing but looked into Terence's eyes as if reading there the squire's indefinable anxieties.

"But I'm worried," Terence continued. "And I've come to ask you something."

Guinglain's gaze shifted to a spot over Terence's shoulder, and an expression of curiosity flickered across his face. "Could we talk about it in a moment?" he asked. "I'm about to have some visitors, people I've never met before."

Terence turned, and at first saw nothing. Then he heard a crunch of gravel under a person's foot and, a few seconds later, watched a young man and woman step from the forest. The young woman carried a swaddled infant in her arms. Both looked haggard and drawn. Guinglain left Terence and walked across the yard to meet them. "Good afternoon, friends," he said. "Welcome."

"Are you the hermit here?" asked the young man. His voice was gruff, but his eyes seemed beseeching rather than stern.

"I am Brother Guinglain, yes."

"You're very young," the man said.

"Yes."

The woman looked at the man's face, then at Guinglain's, then back at the man's. She said nothing but somehow managed to communicate a message. The man nodded. "They say in the village that you can see things no one else sees. Angels and demons and such."

Guinglain said nothing, waiting.

"So we brought you our baby," the man said, his voice growing harsher. Reaching across to the bundle in the woman's arms, he twitched the blankets back from where the baby's head was and said harshly, "Look at him!"

From where he stood, Terence couldn't see the child's face, but from the way that both parents looked once then averted their eyes, he gathered that there was some deformity there. Guinglain looked calmly at the baby.

"They say in the village that it's a mark of the devil!" the man said hoarsely. "Is it? Did we give birth to a demon? Why? For what sin? What had we done? Why are we being punished?"

For a long moment Guinglain said nothing, then he stretched out his hands, and in a slow, almost stammering voice he said, "Please, may I hold him?" The woman blinked but obediently handed the infant to Guinglain. "What is his name?"

"We've given him no name," the man said.

Faintly, the woman spoke for the first time. "Before he was born, I had thought to name him Thomas."

"Thomas," Guinglain repeated, still gazing into the child's face. At last he looked up at the two young parents. "How came you by this honor?" he breathed. The parents only stared, and slowly Guinglain sank to his knees before them. "This child," he said, "he is . . . he has . . . there is in him a spark of God's own fire, the very image of God's form. He is . . . I have never beheld a soul of greater beauty. Tell me! Who are you?"

The man's jaw had grown slack, but at length he stammered, "I-I am called Rogan, and this is my wife, Margary."

"Rogan and Margary," Guinglain said, his eyes still on them, "I do not know what goodness God has seen in you to give you care of Thomas, but it must be great." Looking around quickly, Guinglain called out, "Children! Come here at once!"

All the children stopped what they were doing and gathered around the kneeling hermit. Terence stepped closer as well and saw that the infant in Guinglain's arms had a black birthmark covering half of its face. The eye within the mark was unnaturally filmy, and Terence guessed that that eye at least was sightless.

"Do you see this child?" Guinglain said to the children eagerly. They did. Every child stared at the infant with a revulsed fascination. "Watch him as he grows!

God has marvelous plans for this Thomas! He will know things that none of us can ever know. Do you hear me?"

All the children nodded, and Guinglain looked back at Rogan and Margary. "You have been given a difficult task," he said. "There are those who will persecute you and the holy Thomas, those who will be cruel and will heap all sorts of abuse on you. But God must have seen great strength in you. I am honored to have met you."

Rogan and Margary looked at each other, speechless.

"And please," Guinglain said, slowly rising to his feet and reluctantly handing Thomas back to his mother, "will you bring him to me again? My hermitage is made more holy by his presence."

A minute later the dazed couple had gone and the children had returned to their former occupations. Terence looked into Guinglain's serene eyes. "And did you really see the image of God's beauty in that child?"

"Of course," Guinglain replied. The corners of his lips curled up very slightly, and in a softer voice, he added, "I see it in every child."

"And in every adult?" Terence asked.

Guinglain's smile changed to a rueful grin. "I think it might be there in every adult," he said, "but I can't always see it."

"That's why I'm here, actually," Terence said. "I want to ask you about someone you mentioned once." Guinglain nodded and Terence continued. "Didn't you tell Gawain and me, back when we were traveling together, that you had met a young man named Mordred?"

Guinglain's face grew somber. "Yes," he said.

"And what did you see in this Mordred's soul?"

Guinglain was silent for a long moment. "I couldn't see Mordred's soul. It was entirely hidden."

"What do you mean?"

"When he spoke, it was with bitterness and mockery," Guinglain said. "But even then I couldn't tell if the words he spoke came from himself or from somewhere else. He made me feel very cold."

Terence nodded. "I know. I felt the same thing, even though when I talked with him, he was very agreeable."

"You've talked with Mordred?"

Terence nodded. "He came to Arthur last week, asking to be received into the Fellowship of the Round Table. There's a meeting in five days to hear him."

Guinglain said solemnly, "In my travels, both in your world and in this one, I have seen great evil. But I have never felt such emptiness as I felt when I was with Mordred. I have to believe that people can change, but Mordred . . . I think you should be frightened, my friend."

Terence swung back into his horse's saddle. "I need to start back to Camelot," he said.

Gawain was playing cards with Kai by a dying fire when Terence stepped into their rooms. Judging from the hour, the two empty pitchers on the floor, and the neglected state of the coals, Terence guessed that both were more than a little in their cups, so he greeted them only briefly and went to bed. It wasn't until just before noon the next day, when Gawain dragged himself blearily from his bedchamber, that Terence had a chance to talk with him.

"I *thought* you came in last night," Gawain said, evidently pleased with this feat of memory. "Do you feel better after your ride?"

"I imagine I feel better than you do," Terence said. "Want something to eat?"

Gawain made a face. "Please don't speak of food to me," he said. "Where did you go?"

"I went to see Guinglain," Terence said.

"The devil you did!" Gawain exclaimed. "I wish you'd told me! I'd have gone with you."

"Sorry, milord. I wanted to be alone this time."

Gawain frowned for a moment. "You went all the way to Guinglain's hermitage and back in . . . what is it, a week? Ten days? How long did you stay?"

"About twenty minutes," Terence replied. "Listen, is that young fellow Mordred still about?"

"You traveled all that way and then stayed —"

"Mordred," Terence repeated. "Have you seen him around?"

"Have I seen him around?" Gawain snorted. "He's like part of the family now. He and Agrivaine are thick as thieves." Agrivaine was the middle born of Gawain's three younger brothers. Gawain shook his head. "Which is odd, really. Mordred always seems pleasant enough — can't imagine why he'd chum around with a wet blanket like Agrivaine. Oh, and my cousins Florence and Lovel showed up at court a day or so after you left, and he's made friends with them, too."

"The Table hasn't met to hear Mordred's case, has it?"

"No, that's tomorrow . . . No, wait: today isn't yesterday anymore, is it?"

Terence sighed. "It hardly ever is, milord."

"Leave me alone. I'm new at this day and haven't got the hang of it yet. The Table is meeting this afternoon." Terence relaxed. He had made it in time, though just barely. "So how's Guinglain?"

"He's very happy," Terence said. "More than anyone I've ever met."

"Happy and a holy man, too," muttered Gawain. "Who'd have thought it? Well, I'm glad things are going well for him."

It occurred to Terence that Guinglain's happiness had nothing to do with how well things went for him, but he decided not to try explaining that to Gawain at the moment. "Whether you think it or not," Terence said, "you'll feel better with some food in your stomach."

Gawain grumbled something indistinguishable, but he took the small loaf of brown bread that Terence had brought him from the castle kitchens and began to chew. Terence left him alone and went to see Eileen. She was in her sitting room with Sarah, both sewing, when Terence swung through the window. Sarah jumped with obvious alarm. "Oh, it's you," she said.

"Welcome home, Terence," Eileen said, smiling warmly. "When did you arrive?"

"Last night after midnight," he said.

"Do you *always* come in that way?" Sarah demanded. "You scared me."

"You really *should* be careful," Eileen pointed out. "After all, I've got a guest here. What if Sarah had been dressing?"

"I knocked earlier," Terence said, "but no one answered." He glanced at the door, noting with mild surprise that it was bolted with a heavy wooden beam.

"Was that you?" Sarah asked. "Oh, I'm sorry. I thought it was Alexander."

Terence grinned. "What, the emperor of Constantinople? Is he still around?"

"He says he won't leave without Sarah," Eileen explained.

"I see," Terence said, keeping his face bland. "So are you betrothed yet?"

"No, and shut up," Sarah said. "I don't want to hear it."

"Hear what?" Terence protested. "I wasn't going to say a thing."

"If that's true, then you're the only one," Sarah muttered.

Eileen laid down her needlework. "Many people at court have felt the need to tell Sarah what a brilliant match it would be," she said.

"Just in case I hadn't realized it for myself," Sarah added.

"Well, have you turned him down?" Terence asked.

Sarah hesitated. "No," she admitted. "I don't love him, but I don't actually dislike him. There are times I think he might not be a bad choice. I believe he's a man of honor, anyway. But I don't like everybody assuming I'll marry him just because he's the emperor."

"And he's still pursuing you?"

Sarah rolled her eyes. "Like a ferret after a rabbit. I try to slow him down by acting cold and putting him off, but that only seems to make him more sure of me than ever."

Terence remembered what Dinadan had said at the tournament about the French traditions of courtly love. It had sounded absurd, but Dinadan was no fool, and he had spent a lot of time traveling on the continent. Perhaps he was right. "Maybe he thinks you're just being discreet by pretending not to love him."

"That what he keeps saying," Sarah said. "It's what puts me most out of patience with him, because it gives me no answer. If I encourage him, he believes that I love him. If I don't encourage him, he believes it even more. He says he wants to do great deeds for me, to slay my enemies."

"Very romantic," Terence said drily. "And how do you reply?"

"I told him I had already slain them all myself. He didn't believe me."

A new thought occurred to Terence. "Say, how does that old advisor of Alexander's feel about this? Acor-something."

"Acoriondes," Eileen said. "And he's just three years older than I am, dear."

Terence closed his eyes. "I meant 'that youthful courtier.'"

"He's the only one on my side," Sarah said. "He doesn't say anything, but I can tell he's hoping I'll stand firm."

"It's probably part of his job to protect Alexander from unwise marriages," Terence reflected. Sarah's eyebrows lifted haughtily, and Terence added hurriedly, "I mean from a diplomatic point of view. Kings aren't supposed to marry for love; they have to make marriages that will help their states. Even Arthur's marriage with Guinevere was an alliance between him and old King Leodegrance."

"But Arthur and Guinevere love each other," Sarah pointed out.

"They do now," Terence agreed, "but it was a bit rocky at first." Changing the subject, Terence turned to

Eileen. "Can you tell me anything about this new fellow, Mordred? Have you met him?"

"Once or twice," Eileen replied. "Seems nice enough. Why do you ask?"

Terence hesitated. So far, everyone's impression of Mordred seemed to be favorable. "Just thinking ahead to the meeting of the Table this afternoon," Terence said.

In past years King Arthur's Round Table, the great council of equals, had been the place where he and his knights had come together to decide how to face some enemy or challenge. Now, having fewer of both, the Table met rarely and with less critical issues. This day, there were only three or four small matters to resolve, which were dealt with quickly, before Arthur said, "And finally, we have a knight making application to join our fellowship. Over the past week or two, most of you have gotten to know young Mordred. Mordred, would you stand, please?"

Only knights of the fellowship had seats at the table, so Mordred been sitting against the back wall with the handful of nonknightly counselors who were admitted to the meetings of the Table, near Terence. Now he rose diffidently to his feet. "Here, Your Highness."

"Tell us, Mordred, why you wish to join our number."

Mordred smiled — a very attractive smile, too, Terence noted — and said, "I suppose you have to ask, sire, but really! Every child born in England dreams of joining your fellowship. Since I was a child being raised alone by my mother, I have dreamt that one day I might be a part of this collection of heroes, doing my part to make England great."

"You were raised by your mother?" asked the king.

"Yes, Your Highness."

"What happened to your father?"

Mordred took a breath, then said, "I never knew him, sire. Nor has he ever known me. I suppose I must tell the story. You see, twenty years ago, my mother was rescued from a dragon by a great knight."

Several voices interrupted Mordred's narrative. "A dragon! Did he say a *dragon?*"

"That's what Mother says," Mordred continued. "She had come upon the beast in a forest clearing, and it had just started toward her when this knight rode up and attacked. Killed it, too, in hard fighting. Well, the knight was wounded in the fight, and so my mother took him home to care for him. For several days, he was feverish, but my mother knew a little about healing herbs, and she saved his life. She fell in love with him, of course, and before the knight left, they . . . well, I was born nine months later."

Arthur's face was still. "And do you know who this knight was?"

Mordred shook his head. "Mother says he wouldn't tell his name. All she could tell is that he wore black armor and that he didn't seem very happy. Actually, the way Mother said it was 'He bore a secret grief.' Mother talked like that."

"Have you ever tried to find your father?"

Mordred shrugged. "I used to think about it sometimes, but I don't anymore. I don't really have any quarrel with him. It isn't his fault that he didn't return Mother's love. The fellow probably saved dozens of damsels in his life, and he couldn't fall in love with all of them. I suppose he shouldn't have taken advantage of Mother, but I won't judge him. I imagine in her younger days Mother was quite a beauty. And she *had* just saved his life."

"Ah, yes," said the king. "And where exactly was this knight wounded?"

"I think Mother said it was his shoulder. The left one, maybe. I'm not sure."

The king leaned back in his chair and gazed thoughtfully at Mordred. In the silence, Sir Griflet, an aging knight wearing a doublet of a preposterous shade of pink, said, "Well, really! A dragon! I mean, it doesn't sound very likely, does it? *I've* never seen a dragon, and I've been a knight for nearly thirty years."

Several others nodded. Stories about knights slaying dragons were commonplace, but dragons themselves were not. Kai growled, "I wonder if *any* of you has seen a dragon."

After a moment, Gawain cleared his throat. "One,"

he said. "Remember, Tor?" Sir Tor, across the table, nodded, and Gawain continued. "Of course, it wasn't a real dragon: it was my dear aunt, Morgan Le Fay, taking a different form by sorcery. But we still saw one. And I suppose this dragon could have been part of an enchantment, too, don't you think?"

Gawain looked inquiringly at Mordred, who shrugged and smiled. "I suppose. I wasn't around yet, you know, so I really couldn't say."

"I have another question for Mordred," asked Dinadan suddenly. "If your story is true, why would no one have heard of it? A knight who saves a damsel from a dragon — well, why in heaven's name would he keep that to himself? It's rather a good tale."

"I don't know," Mordred replied thoughtfully. "Maybe the knight didn't think anyone would believe him." Mordred's smile faded, and he looked around the room. "After all, most of you don't believe me."

"Is your mother still alive?" Arthur asked.

Mordred shook his head sadly. "No. She died of a fever last month."

The king nodded. "I'm sorry, lad," he said softly. Then, in a firmer voice, he said, "We have heard a curious tale today. Some of you may still not believe it, but you shall have to decide that at another time. In the end, the story of the dragon has nothing to do with Mordred's request. Mordred, at this table we receive only those who have already proven themselves by some act of bravery. Setting aside what your father did, have you done any deeds yourself that are worthy of knighthood?"

Mordred shook his head. "I'm afraid not," he said frankly. "And, to be perfectly honest, I'm not all that skilled a swordsman, either."

"Nothing wrong with that," murmured Dinadan, which drew a laugh from the other knights. Dinadan was respected for several things, not one of which was his swordsmanship.

The king smiled faintly. "And what, may I ask, *are* you skilled at?"

Mordred hesitated. "Well, it doesn't sound very dramatic, but I've always been good with people — helping them smooth out their differences and make friends again, that sort of thing."

As Mordred said this, his face assumed an expression of limpid openness and honesty, and once again Terence felt that dread chill begin in his heart and slowly spread throughout his breast.

King Arthur smiled widely. "Don't be ashamed of that, lad. In these times of peace, I have more than enough swordsmen. But I could always use a diplomat."

"But . . . but could a person earn knighthood like that?" stammered Mordred.

"I don't know why saving lives by stopping a war should be less honorable than saving lives with the sword," Arthur said. "I cannot grant your request now, but I earnestly beg you to remain at Camelot. When an opportunity arises for you to prove yourself, you shall be given your chance."

Most of the knights nodded agreement at the king's decision, and Mordred was dismissed from the meeting.

"What do you think, friends?" the king asked.

"I still don't believe the dragon story," Sir Griflet complained.

"It doesn't matter either way," Arthur replied. "Even if the story's untrue, the boy is only repeating what he was told by his mother. It does him no disservice in my eyes that he takes her word. And, as Gawain has pointed out, it *could* be true. No, what I'm asking is, what do you think of the boy?"

"He seems a good lad," Gawain commented. "Frank and honest. He didn't *have* to tell us he wasn't much with a sword."

Several others agreed. Sir Bors said, "Indeed, I like him. It seemed to me that at every question, every challenge, he said *exactly* the right thing."

"And that doesn't bother you?" asked Kai suddenly.

"Eh?" replied Sir Bors.

"When someone always says the right thing, don't you wonder if it wasn't planned that way?"

"And why not?" demanded Agrivaine. "Don't *you* always mean to say the right thing?"

"No," Kai replied abruptly. "I say what I think. And

what I think is that the boy's too good to be true. That's suspicious."

"But you think everything's suspicious," snorted Agrivaine.

"There's some truth in that, you know, Kai," Arthur said gently. "Let us not condemn the boy for being better than expected. As for his saying the right thing, he told us himself that his skill is in diplomacy."

The meeting dispersed a few minutes later, and Terence left, his heart still unnaturally cold and heavy in his breast. Except for Kai's comments, which had sounded surly and peevish even to Terence's ears, no one had had anything bad to say about young Mordred. Terence felt suddenly helpless, realizing that he could say nothing against Mordred that anyone would listen to. His own suspicions of Mordred were based on his and Guinglain's deep feelings, not on anything that could be considered proof. Why is it, Terence wondered, that the things you know most surely are always the things you can't demonstrate to anyone else?

Deciding he would just have to keep an eye on Mordred, Terence returned to his chambers to find Gawain awaiting him. "There you are. Come on. Arthur wants us."

"What for?"

"He just sent Kai to find the two of us and Lancelot. We're to meet him in his own chambers at once."

When they arrived, Terence found not only Arthur, Kai, and Lancelot, but also Queen Guinevere waiting for them. "Shut the door behind you," Arthur said. "And bar it."

Terence obeyed in silence, but his mind and senses were unnaturally alert. The king looked somber, but in another way agitated.

"What's wrong, Arthur?" Guinevere asked. "What's going on?"

"I need to talk about something, something that we never speak of."

"What, my king?" asked Lancelot.

"About the affair that you and Guinevere had when you first came to court."

"Arthur!" exclaimed Guinevere, glancing sharply at the others in the room.

"They all know, my love," Arthur said.

"But all that's over now," Guinevere said. "I am sorry. I was young. I thought . . . I was foolish. Why must we talk about it again? I wish it were forgotten!"

Now Lancelot spoke. "The queen is right. That . . . that episode is over. We both rejected it, and we have both been restored to your favor. Surely you do not suspect —"

"I suspect nothing," the king said. "And I don't bring it up to accuse either of you. You are the love of my life, Gwen, and Lancelot, you are among my most trusted friends. Whatever happened has been forgiven."

"But not forgotten?" asked Lancelot.

"Please, Lance," Arthur said. "Let me finish. When the two of you were — well, during that time — I was driven to distraction, watching you. Maybe some of you remember how I was." Terence and Gawain and Kai all nodded. "To relieve my anguish, and maybe anger, I took to going out on quests alone."

Guinevere's eyes grew wide. "What? But I don't remember —"

"I told you I was going to a monastery for prayer and meditation," Arthur explained, a little sheepishly. "But what I was really doing was challenging every knight I met to combat, then bashing them about. It made me feel better. Only Kai knew what I was really doing. Oh, and Terence."

Gawain blinked. "You knew this, Terence?"

"I was one of the knights that got bashed about," Terence explained. "Back when you were trying to convince me to become a knight and making me practice jousting and such. Arthur found me working at it alone one day and, um, gave me a private lesson."

"But one day, on one of these quests," Arthur went on, "I actually did something worth doing. I was riding alone, as usual, and heard a woman scream. I rode toward the sound and found her in a clearing, about to be attacked by a . . . a dragon."

Terence froze, feeling something horrible and inevitable clutch at him. Mordred! The knights were motionless as well. Only Guinevere, who hadn't been at the meeting of the Round Table, responded to this. "A dragon! Really?"

Arthur nodded, his eyes meeting those of the other men, each in turn. "As for the rest, it happened much as young Mordred said. I fought the dragon, killed it, and rescued the damsel — and he was right about her, too: she was very beautiful. She cared for my wounds."

"You were hurt?" exclaimed the queen.

Arthur lifted a sleeve and showed them a long white scar on his left shoulder. "In a few days I was well enough to ride, and I told her I would be going the next morning. She cried and begged me to stay."

"Did she know who you were?" Guinevere demanded.

Arthur shook his head. "I never told her my name," he said, "not even when we . . . well, as it seems, when we conceived a son."

"Oh, Arthur," the queen said softly.

Kai scowled at her and snapped, "What did you expect, Gwen?"

"Enough, Kai!" the king said sharply.

"And you never told me?" Guinevere whispered.

"When we began trying to put our marriage back together, it was so hard. I thought this would only make things worse."

Guinevere's eyes blurred, but she forced herself to meet the king's gaze and say, "I love you, Arthur."

"And I you, Gwen. But that's not all," Arthur said. Guinevere's eyes grew wide again, and she clutched her hands together. "Today I learned that son's name: Mordred."

"Mordred," Guinevere whispered. "That boy who . . . he's your son?"

"He told the story to the fellowship today."

"Then everyone knows?" Guinevere asked, her voice growing shrill.

"Only those in this room know who that knight was," Arthur said calmly. "But that's why I asked you here. I think . . . I think I would like to claim him publicly."

"Arthur, no!" The queen's tone was frantic. "For all these years we've told no one of my — about Lancelot and me. I've lived in fear that people would find out. I couldn't face it! You can't shame me like this! I've never betrayed you since then. I never will. Please."

"Your Highness," Gawain said gently to the queen, "the past hasn't been forgotten. People still tell stories about you and Lancelot. Not here, of course, but in other —"

"I know," the queen said, her voice growing wilder. "But as long as we don't admit it here, it's just a story. Arthur, if you admit to fathering a child with another woman, how will it make me look? And you, too! You'll be dishonored as much as I am!"

Arthur's face looked gray and old. Lancelot stared at

the floor. Kai and Gawain exchanged glances, and all Terence could think was *Please, don't make Mordred the heir to your throne! Please, no!*

Slowly Arthur nodded to the queen. "I will say nothing without your permission."

4

The Wooing of Lady Sarah

Public or not, King Arthur's relationship to Mordred complicated matters and only reaffirmed Terence's resolve to keep an eye on Mordred, starting the next morning. That wasn't so easy, though, on account of the acrobats and jugglers and minstrels that had suddenly filled the court.

Terence became aware of these performers shortly after breakfast, when snatches of music began to filter into his and Gawain's rooms from the small court outside their door. Stepping outside, Terence found a crowd listening appreciatively to a band of seven or eight musicians, all with different instruments, playing in the square. Slipping through the throng, Terence made his way to the front, where he found Dinadan. "What's all this?" Terence whispered.

"Shhh," Dinadan hissed back. A moment later, though, when the musicians finished the song they had been playing, he turned to Terence and said, "Wonderful, isn't it?"

"Who are they?"

"Haven't any idea. They just showed up this morning and began playing. They're all good, but having them all together like that, in harmony — absolutely splendid!"

A courtier in the crowd tossed a coin to the musicians, the usual tribute for wandering minstrels, but one of the musicians laid down his rebec, took up the coin, and threw it back to the courtier. "Nay, sir," the musician said. "We do not play for money but for love."

"Hard to spend love at a tavern!" called someone.

The crowd chuckled, but the musician went on, "If you wish to gratify us, do not give us money, but help us. Tell the beautiful Lady Sarah of Milrick that a heart lies at her feet, waiting for her to take it up."

"Eeugh," said Dinadan.

The musician retrieved his instrument, and the musicians began a new song. Terence slipped away, leaving Dinadan enraptured by the music and the crowd delighted by the romance.

In the main courtyard by the front gate, Terence came upon another crowd. Spotting Kai at the fringes, watching from atop a low wall, Terence skirted the throng and joined him. "What's to do here?" he asked.

"Blasted mummers," snorted Kai.

Terence followed his gaze and, at the center of the yard, made out several masked forms waving their arms and leaping gracefully in the air. Mummers — silent actors — were often to be found at the Christmas season, acting out the story of the nativity, but Terence didn't remember seeing them in summer before. "What are they presenting?"

"Before they started, a herald announced that they'd be showing us 'The Allegory of the Rose,' a tale of love."

"Oh," Terence said. "So, what's it about?"

"Geldings in tight clothes, apparently."

Guessing that there was more to 'The Allegory of the Rose' than Kai's interpretation, Terence slipped off the wall and moved closer. There were three mummers, one of them prancing in a circle, and the other two twisted into a knot. Terence watched for a while but understood none of it. Evidently, his confusion was shared. After a few moments, a man standing beside Terence said to his neighbor, "Here, Jem, I think I got it. Those two in the bundle are a flower. They must be the rose."

His friend, Jem, considered this. "Mebbe," he said. "Unless they're the allegory."

"Aren't allegories long and skinny? Like snap-dragons?"

"Depends on the variety," Jem said sagely.

They watched in silence for another minute. Then the first man said, "Mebbe it's a pansy."

"Ay, that'd be it."

Terence backed out of the crowd and walked away. A minute later, he came upon a brightly dressed minstrel, seated in a doorway strumming at a lute. As Terence approached, he raised his voice:

> *"I sing in praise of lovely Sarah,*
> *In all the earth is there one faireh?*
> *Her eyes are stars, her smile the sun,*
> *To be her mirror, rivers run.*
> *The flowers fade before her cheeks,*
> *Compared to her, they smell like leeks . . ."*

Terence moved on quickly. Over the next ten minutes he found two more minstrels, a band of acrobats engaged in spelling out the name Sarah with their bodies, and a juggler who chattered all through his presentation about how the balls and other objects he kept in the air represented such things as purity and faithfulness and humble service to the fair Sarah. The atmosphere at court was like a St. Bartholomew's Day fair, and various enterprising townspeople were already setting up stalls to sell their wares to the gawking crowds, adding to the general confusion. Off to one side, out of the bustle, Terence made out the slim form of Alexander's counselor, Acoriondes, watching from beside the stables. Skirting a troupe of dancers, Terence joined him.

"Good morning, sir," Terence said.

Acoriondes nodded. "Good morning, Squire Terence. I did not know you were back at Camelot."

"I returned two nights ago," Terence replied. He indicated the dancers with a nod. "All this must have cost your master a great deal of money and bother."

Acoriondes started to speak, then closed his mouth again.

Terence waited a moment, then asked, "Out of curiosity, what does he expect to accomplish?"

A pained expression flitted across Acoriondes's face. "None of this is my master's doing. The emperor's only mistake — a grave mistake in my estimation — was in giving his brother, Cligés, permission to arrange these displays of love. Cligés swears that this is the usual way of courtship at Camelot. All the tales say this. Is it indeed so?"

Terence grinned. "No," he said.

"I see," Acoriondes murmured. For a minute he seemed lost in thought. Then, abruptly, he asked, "Forgive me for prying, but since our arrival here I have heard much about you and your adventures with Sir Gawain. I have also heard that you are a friend of Lady Sarah's. Is this so?"

"Yes."

"From your knowledge of the lady, do you imagine

that these, ah, performances will spark love in her heart?"

Terence grinned more broadly. "From what I know of Sarah, I wouldn't think so." Then, guessing where Acoriondes was leading, he added, "But I might be able to drop by her rooms and find out for certain."

Acoriondes nodded slowly. "I admit that's what I was hoping. But I should warn you that visiting Lady Sarah may be difficult. My understanding is that she has bolted her door against the footmen in the corridor."

"Footmen?"

"Footmen," Acoriondes repeated, his face blank. "There are, I believe, a half-dozen footmen waiting outside her door, each with a large sack filled with rose petals."

"Rose petals," Terence repeated blankly.

"To strew at her feet wherever she walks."

"You're . . . you're joking," Terence said, his lips curving in a smile of pure delight as he pictured Sarah striding through Camelot with petal-tossing servants trotting at her side.

Acoriondes sighed. "I fear not," he said.

"Oh, I definitely need to visit with Sarah," Terence said.

"And Squire Terence," Acoriondes said slowly, "I wonder if I might ask a favor of you. My master truly believes that all this confusion will influence Lady

Sarah's heart in his favor. If he is mistaken, I should like very much to know that."

Terence nodded. "I'll let you know," he promised.

He didn't even try going to Eileen and Sarah's door but went at once to the back window and dropped in. Eileen was sitting alone by the fire. "Hello, love," Terence said.

"I wouldn't say that word too loudly," Eileen commented. "Sarah's gone off it just now."

Terence nodded. "And where is the famous Sarah, than whom there is no one faireh?"

"In the bedroom, putting salve on her hands." Terence waited patiently, and after a second Eileen dimpled. "She skinned her knuckles, you see."

"On what?"

"On the teeth and noses of some gentlemen that she found in the corridor."

"Gentlemen who were sprinkling rose petals at her feet?"

"No! Is that what they're up to?" Eileen asked, her control breaking down as she dissolved in laughter.

"Are the footmen all right?" Terence asked.

"They'll live. I pulled Sarah off them after a bit. After all, she didn't really want to hit them; she wants to hit Alexander."

"No, I don't," came Sarah's muffled voice through the bedroom door. "Alexander I want to flay with a dull knife." A moment later she stormed into the room, her hands wrapped in fresh cloths. "What an ass! To think all this foofaraw would make me love him!"

Mindful of his promise to Acoriondes, Terence said, "Then it doesn't?"

Sarah stared at him. "Are you mad? Would a passel of fool minstrels make *you* love someone?"

"I just wanted to be sure," Terence explained. "Maybe I can help get rid of them for you. Wait here."

Twenty minutes later, having told Acoriondes how Sarah felt, Terence watched the first performers leave Camelot. Acoriondes was nothing if not efficient. Without being at all obvious, he had managed to speak privately to every minstrel, mummer, and musician, and within moments of his talking to them, they began packing up to leave. With the performers gone, the crowds dispersed, and an hour later Camelot was back to normal. Terence turned to go tell Sarah it was safe to leave her rooms again, but he was stopped by a quiet voice at his elbow.

"I thank you again, Squire Terence." It was Acoriondes.

"You're welcome."

For a moment Acoriondes didn't speak. Then he said, "Squire Terence?"

"Yes?"

"I would not have you think that my master is a fool. He is not. He has trusted too much in his brother, who in turn has trusted too much in foolish stories, but Alexander is a good man, great of heart. He is the best master I have ever served, and he will be a great emperor when he is older."

Terence nodded, then asked, "And why are you telling all this to a mere squire?"

"I told you that I had learned much about you. While you were away this past week, I have heard many stories about you, and of one thing I am certain. You are not a mere squire."

Terence grinned. "Be careful not to trust too much in foolish stories."

With genuine amusement, Acoriondes returned Terence's smile, the solemn courtier's face seeming suddenly years younger.

What with helping Acoriondes get rid of what the court was already beginning to call the Festival of St. Sarah, Terence had had no chance to watch Mordred, and at dinner that evening the young man was nowhere to be found. No one knew the goings-on at court better than Kai, so as soon as he was able, Terence caught the seneschal's eye and gestured for him to step aside with him. "Where's that fellow Mordred?" Terence hissed as soon as they were alone.

Kai peered at him shrewdly. "You don't like him either, do you?"

"Where is he?"

"Gone," Kai replied bluntly. "On his first quest, you might say."

Terence blinked. King Arthur sent his knights out on quests to fight injustice or drive away bandits, but there had been no reports of such problems for months. "A quest?"

"It's what you might call a diplomatic quest," growled Kai. "About midmorning today, a messenger arrived, reporting that Count Anders has refused to pay his taxes again." Count Anders was a powerful nobleman from East Anglia who was a recurring annoyance to the king. It wasn't that he was actively rebellious. He had sworn an oath of fealty to the king, like every other vassal. But he was always the last of the king's nobles to perform his lawful duties. Just a few months before, King Arthur had had to send an army to collect his rents. Kai continued, "So nothing would do for Arthur but to send Mordred off to deal with him, to see if diplomacy would work better than a show of force."

"He sent that boy alone on a mission like that?" Terence gasped.

"Nay, Bedivere's with him," Kai admitted. "But Arthur made it clear that he wanted Mordred to talk to Anders first." Terence shook his head. It didn't seem like a job for a youth. Anders was a slippery, conniving fellow, not to be trusted. "I know," Kai muttered, lowering his voice. "But Arthur's never had a son before."

80

They were interrupted by a commotion in the banquet hall behind them, and Terence and Kai returned to their places as Emperor Alexander's party entered the hall. As Terence took his spot behind Gawain's chair, Alexander was kneeling before a tight-lipped Sarah, apologizing brokenly to her. "It is that I am unable to speak my love for you, Lady Sarah. Even in my own tongue, I am not a man of well speeches, and in the English, I cannot say all that is in my heart. I wished the singers to speak my love for me. If it was not well done of me, then I ask your forgiveness. My hope was to praise you, not shame you. Forgive me?"

Sarah glowered at him for a moment, then said, "Oh, get up, Alexander. Just don't do it again."

The emperor sighed with relief, then smiled impishly. "I will obey you, my lady. From fear as much as from love. I do not wish to be treated as you treated my footmen."

Even Sarah had to join in the ensuing laughter, and Terence reflected that as maladroit as Alexander could be, it was impossible not to like the emperor.

Over the next two weeks, the emperor didn't make a spectacle of his love, but no one could doubt that he was pursuing Sarah as ardently as ever. In every way, he was attentive to her needs — or what he imagined to be her needs. When she went riding with Eileen, Alexander was there to help her mount her horse.

When she walked to the town, one of the emperor's own footmen followed her (at a safe distance), ready to carry anything she purchased or to run errands for her. When she spoke in Alexander's presence, he immediately turned his attention from everyone else and listened to her. Sarah showed no sign of weakening, but as the days passed Alexander won nearly everyone else's heart. That Sarah still held out against so eligible and determined a suitor struck almost everyone as both foolish and cruel.

"Why *do* you refuse Alexander, anyway?" Eileen asked one evening, as she and Sarah and Terence sat behind barred door.

"Oh, don't you start, too," Sarah sighed. "I'm getting enough of that from Guinevere, who thinks it's all *so* romantic."

"But why?" Eileen persisted. "You don't dislike him. Of that I'm sure."

Sarah hesitated. "No," she admitted. "I don't. I might even one day learn to love him. But I don't yet."

"So you like him and think you would probably learn to love him. That's a more promising beginning than many marriages start with," Eileen commented.

"I know. But I don't want to settle for *probably*." She drew a breath. "Remember, as a child I saw everyone I loved murdered. It makes you careful, about loving people. This isn't easy for me."

A gentle rap came from the chamber door. Sarah

seemed to sag, but Eileen met Terence's eyes and jerked her head at the entrance. Terence drew the bolt and opened the door to reveal Alexander's younger brother, Cligés. "Please," Cligés said. "I speak for my brother."

"Come in," Terence said.

Cligés entered, his hat in his hand. "I . . . I am sorry for disturbing," he stammered, kneeling before Sarah.

"What do you want?" Sarah asked, but her voice was not unkind.

"Alexandros asks please if you . . . love another."

"If I . . . oh, I see," Sarah said.

"If you love another," Cligés said, "Alexandros will —" Cligés consulted a scrap of paper on which several words were written in Greek letters. "— honor your love. He will say no more to you."

Sarah hesitated, then nodded to herself. "It's an honest question. No, Cligés, you may tell your brother that I do not love another."

Cligés's face broke into a dazzling smile. "Then he may hope?"

Sarah gave him a measured gaze. "Tell Alexander that he must wait. But yes, he may hope."

Cligés thanked her profusely, then hurried away with his message. Terence barred the door again.

"Do you know what I need?" Sarah asked plaintively. "I need to take a trip somewhere. Just to get away."

"Where?" asked Eileen.

"The antipodes, maybe. Africa, at least. What's farthest from here?"

The next morning, Mordred and Bedivere returned from their diplomatic mission, with Count Anders riding between them. Arthur received his stubborn vassal in the throne room, where the count knelt before the king and laid a wooden chest at the foot of the throne. "My taxes, sire, along with my rents for the next quarter," he said.

"Your rents, too?" asked Arthur, mildly surprised.

"I have not been as true to my vows as I could have been, Your Highness. But your ambassador has persuaded me to amend my ways."

Arthur looked at Mordred, standing humbly at the rear of the room, and a smile touched the king's lips. "Indeed? And what did Mordred say that accomplished what so many others have failed to do?"

"It was not what he said, sire. It was that he listened."

The king raised his eyebrows. "Listened to what?"

Mordred stepped forward. "Please, Your Highness, if I may explain?" Arthur nodded. "Count Anders has been slow to pay his lawful dues because of his own worry. His lands lie on England's eastern shore, and he had heard rumors that pirates from across the sea were planning to attack. He needed every farthing to fortify the coasts. I simply reminded him that the defense of

England was not his job but yours, and that by setting himself against you he was depriving himself of his greatest ally."

Kai, standing behind Arthur, looked skeptical, but Arthur nodded. "Mordred is right. I should be glad to discuss your defenses and determine what is to be done."

The count bowed again, and the general court was dismissed while Arthur and his council of war met with Count Anders. Terence was not a part of that council, but he heard the results when Gawain returned to their rooms later. Arthur had agreed to send a caravan of supplies, horses, and weapons to fortify Count Anders's coastal defenses, and Count Anders had renewed his oath of vassalage to the king. "It seems to have worked out pretty well," Gawain concluded, "in spite of all Kai could say."

"Kai didn't like it?"

"He says he's not keen on giving weapons to someone who just a few months ago looked to be starting a rebellion."

"Well, that's a fair point, I'd think," Terence said.

Gawain shrugged. "Maybe, but it was pretty clear that Kai's real reason was that he doesn't like Mordred. I must say, Mordred took it pretty calmly, too."

"Mordred was there? In the war council?"

Gawain nodded. "A little irregular, I know, but he'd begun the negotiations, after all."

Terence nodded, but he couldn't help wondering if Arthur was granting Mordred so much trust only because he so desperately wanted him to be trustworthy. Somehow it didn't seem enough to believe something was so just because you wanted it to be so. But two days later even Terence was surprised at the extent of Arthur's trust in Mordred. That morning, the king announced that since England was at complete peace, it was time for him to make an overdue visit to the lands under his rule in northern France, in Brittany. He, the queen, the council, and most of his court would spend several months there, and in the king's absence England would be under the charge of Mordred and Sir Bedivere.

5

THE BATTLE OF WINDSOR

The party that set out for Brittany a week later was much larger than usual, and several of those who went with the king would have given much to stay behind. Among those were Kai, Sarah, and Terence.

Brittany, on France's northwestern coast, had belonged to the kings of Britain for as long as anyone could remember. It had often been neglected by those kings, but King Arthur tried to rule all of his lands with equal care, even those that lay across the sea. He had appointed an honest Breton governor and made a point of visiting Brittany himself as often as possible. But those delegations had usually consisted of the king, Sir Bedivere, and an honor guard of a dozen or so knights. In his absence, Arthur had always left Kai in charge of Britain, so his change of plans this time surprised everyone. Not only was he leaving England in the hands of a youth who wasn't even a knight yet, but he specifically named Kai, Gawain, and Terence among those who would go to Brittany with him.

Kai was livid and, in private, argued vehemently against leaving Mordred in charge, even with Bedivere at his side. "You know Bedivere, Arthur," Kai protested. "He's too trusting! Especially of young knights! He's soft!"

"Why do you think I chose him?" was all the king would reply.

For her part, Sarah had seen the king's journey to France as her chance to get away from Alexander and had begged his permission to go along. But the emperor had thwarted these plans in the simplest way: by announcing his decision to accompany the king to Brittany as well.

As for Terence, he was more than ever convinced that he ought to be watching Mordred, but he said nothing to the king until the night before their departure. It was late evening, but the midsummer sun was still above the horizon when Terence happened to glimpse a movement on the north tower. Having for the moment lost track of Mordred, Terence climbed the tower stairs to see who was there. It was King Arthur, standing alone at the turret, examining the lush landscape before him.

"My liege," Terence said. "Forgive my interruption."

"It's all right, Terence," Arthur said. "Looking for Mordred?"

Terence had to smile ruefully. "Yes, actually. Am I that obvious?"

"Not to everyone, I imagine. But to me, yes. You see, I also am keeping an eye on him."

Terence raised one eyebrow. "Are you suspicious of Mordred?"

"I have no reason to be," the king replied evenly. "Have you?"

Terence swallowed. "No," he said at last. "Nothing I could explain. Call it a feeling. I just sense that he's not to be trusted."

"An opinion you share with Kai, it seems," Arthur said drily.

Terence nodded, and for a long moment they looked together at the fields below, glowing red in the blush of the setting sun.

"Terence," the king said, "have you wondered what will happen to England when I'm dead?" Terence nodded. Everyone had wondered. "And what do you foresee?" Arthur continued.

Terence answered frankly. "War. I think that nobles who've been lying low during the peace will try to grab what they can when there's no one on the throne."

The king nodded. "That's what I see, too. And doesn't it seem to you that a true king ought to care as much for the next generation as he does for his own?

But what can I do to prevent such a war? I should be preparing my successor for the evil times to come, but Guinevere and I have no children."

"Couldn't you just choose one of your knights to succeed you?" Terence asked.

"Who?" the king answered. "Who would you choose? It should be someone who's young enough to rule for more than a few years — so not Kai or Bedivere. But it should also be someone with the wisdom and experience to rule well. Can you think of one of the young knights you would choose as king?"

Terence pondered this. He knew of several honorable and trustworthy young knights but could think of none who could step into Arthur's shoes. He shook his head. "But Mordred? You've only known him a few weeks. Surely you haven't chosen him!"

"I have chosen to test him," Arthur replied, "to see if he shows promise. And so far, I think you'll agree, he's exceeded expectations. At least he isn't a hothead who'll rush into war. And there's one more thing. Whoever follows me must be someone the country will accept as king, and Mordred *is* my son. One day, when I die if not before, I will make that known. I may have to hide that truth now, for Guinevere's sake, but I won't take it with me to the grave."

Terence chose his words carefully. "But what if Mordred isn't a man of honor, O king?"

"He still must know who his father is. I have no right

to hide that from him forever. And then what? Once he's known to be my son, the die will be cast. Whoever I choose as my successor, some will declare Mordred king, simply because of his birth. If I don't choose Mordred, I'll be guaranteeing a civil war."

None of this had occurred to Terence before, but he saw that the king was right. As soon as Mordred's birth was known to all, then most would accept his right to the throne without question. Then he frowned. "But, sire, his birth is not legitimate."

"Neither is mine," Arthur replied calmly. "Remember? I'm the bastard son of King Uther Pendragon and Igraine of Cornwall."

Terence nodded. The king's arguments were irrefutable. "But why give Mordred so much responsibility so quickly? Surely there is time to —"

"One never knows how much time one has, Terence," Arthur replied calmly. "I may die sooner than expected." Terence looked sharply at the king's face. Arthur smiled. "Nay, don't look like that, old friend. I have no reason to think that my time is nearing. Call it a feeling."

With this Terence had to be satisfied. "All the same, my liege, I beg you: let me stay at Camelot while you are gone."

Arthur shook his head. "No, Terence. I'm not the only one who is aware that you're watching Mordred: Mordred knows. He probably thinks you're doing so at my command. But this time I want him to feel entirely trusted. Will you obey me in this, Terence?"

Dropping to one knee, Terence bowed his head. "I would throw myself from this tower at your command, my king. Yes, I will obey."

King Arthur shook his head. "Don't be an ass, Terence. If I ever command you to throw yourself from a tower, have me locked up, will you?"

If it weren't for his gnawing anxiety about Mordred, Terence would have enjoyed the time in Brittany. At any rate, everyone else in the British party did. King Arthur and Kai spent every morning with the Breton governor, going over laws and accounts, but even they set business aside at noon. And, for the rest of the delegation, the visit was a time of uninterrupted pleasure. There were games and hawking parties and hunts and banquets and picnics and, of course, courtly dalliance. Gawain, noting how many courtiers and ladies had paired up during the trip, wondered to Terence if it might be something in the French air.

"French wine, more like," Terence replied drily.

"Well, you can't fault them for that. It *is* good wine. These Bretons couldn't make a decent ale to save their lives, which is a pity, but they've compensated nicely with their wines. And it does seem to aid courtship, doesn't it? I wouldn't be surprised if we have a half-dozen weddings once we return to England."

Among the romances, though, Emperor Alexander's pursuit of Sarah remained unquestionably the courtship-in-chief. Alexander missed no opportunity to express his faithful devotion. One day Sarah was overheard to admire a particular flower; the next morning, a dozen bouquets of that flower were delivered to her door. "Fine," she muttered to Eileen and Terence. "I don't like that flower anymore." To make matters worse, Alexander had gained a powerful ally. Queen Guinevere, who had always found the emperor's affection to be moving, began to take an active part in his courtship. She now shared with Cligés the role of advisor and go-between. She took messages to Sarah from her imperial admirer and, in return, delivered tokens to him — things that Sarah had touched, a hair plucked from her brush, an embroidered handkerchief, and so on.

"It's all so false!" Sarah complained to Terence after about three weeks in Brittany. "No, not false. That's not what I mean. I don't think Alexander's *lying*, exactly. But he isn't real, either. Everything he does is like his next move in some game with complicated rules that I don't even want to understand. I thought back at Camelot, when he sent his brother to ask if he could hope, that he was finally going to be open and straightforward. Cligés looked so sincere. But now we're back to all this mummery and nonsense. When are we going back to Britain, anyway?"

As it turned out, they left the very next day. That evening, at a large al fresco banquet in the fields outside the governor's castle, a French minstrel's long and tragic tale of doomed love was interrupted by a flurry of hoofbeats, then a galloping rider. The horseman threw himself from the saddle and ran, gasping, to King Arthur. "My liege!" cried the messenger. "I bring you the worst of news! You are betrayed, and it is my fault!"

It was Mordred.

King Arthur rose to his feet. "What is it?"

"Count Anders has raised a rebellion against you, using the weapons that I convinced you to give him. I was a fool, sire!"

"But where are my armies? I left enough troops to face a rebellion."

"Most are in Scotland. Bedivere got word of an uprising there and sent them to counter it. My king, Anders has already burned London and set up a base somewhere thereabouts."

"Where's Bedivere?" asked the king sharply.

Mordred bowed his head. "A prisoner, my lord. Someone at Camelot must be in the count's pay, because a party of Anders's men got into the castle and captured Bedivere in his bed. But for sheer luck, they would have taken me as well. I was able to kill one and hide."

"But Bedivere's alive, you say?" Arthur looked grim.

"I believe so, sire. I heard one of the men say that

they were to take him to the count. As soon as they were gone, I sent two separate messengers to Scotland, recalling your troops from there. Then I set off for Brittany myself." With a sob, Mordred bowed his face to the ground. "Sire, forgive me. I should have listened to Sir Kai. Count Anders was planning this all along. He played me for a fool, and I didn't see it."

"We have all been fools," the king said. "But tomorrow we shall be warriors. The women shall stay here until I send for them. The rest of us depart at dawn!"

The channel winds cooperated with the British knights' return, with the result that less than a week later Arthur's men had sailed up the Thames River to the old Roman city of London. There they found blackened ruins and grieving citizens, but no Count Anders. The count, they learned, had stayed in London only long enough to pillage it and destroy what was left before moving west, to one of Arthur's secondary residences, Windsor Castle. A day later, Arthur's men were camped across the Thames from the stone walls of Windsor.

Arthur summoned Gawain, Terence, and Mordred to his tent. "I want you to ride to the castle," he said, "and demand Anders's surrender."

"You're sending a delegation?" gasped Kai. "Haven't you had enough of that? You've seen Anders can't be trusted."

"He has Bedivere, remember," Arthur replied calmly. "And even if he didn't, there is no reason to sacrifice more lives. Anders must know he can't win. He has no allies, and my armies — once they're gathered — outnumber his twenty to one. His cause is hopeless."

Gawain shrugged. "We can talk to him, but he won't surrender. He's rebelled against the king; his life is forfeit either way. He'll choose to die in battle. Wouldn't you?"

Arthur nodded. "But we have to try. Ask to speak to Bedivere."

And so Gawain and Mordred put on their armor, crossed the river on the town's ferry, and rode to the front of the castle, with Terence right behind them. "Anders!" shouted Gawain.

He called again, and after a few minutes the count appeared on the battlements. "What do you want?"

"Your surrender!"

"Bugger off!"

"You have no hope!" Gawain called back. "You must see that! Give up now, and some of your men's lives may be spared!"

"What? With no more men than you have over there?" replied the count with a sneer.

It was true that Arthur's present command was small. What had been a large traveling party for a diplomatic mission was much less impressive as a military force. Even taking into account Alexander and his regiment of Greek knights, Arthur had no more than a hundred knights and even fewer foot soldiers.

"Remember who's in that army," Gawain retorted. "Do you count Lancelot as one man? Or Bors? Or Lionel? Or me? Do you imagine that any of us will stop until you are dead?"

Anders appeared to think about this. "I won't talk terms like this, anyway — shouting from a bleeding wall! Send one man to deal with me!"

"What, so you can lock him up with Bedivere? Do you think we're idiots?"

"Wait, Sir Gawain," hissed Mordred.

"What?"

"I'm no fighter. I'll be no loss to the army. Let me go in."

"No. You're mad." Gawain turned back toward Anders.

"This was my fault," Mordred whispered urgently. "Let me see what I can do. If I die, I die. But let me try."

Gawain hesitated, and in that moment of indecision, Mordred called out, "Very well! I'm coming in!" and booted his horse into a gallop. The castle gates opened to admit him, then closed. Gawain and Terence could only stare.

"Something tells me Arthur's not going to be half pleased with this little development," muttered Gawain with a sigh. "Well, on the hundred-to-one chance that

Anders was telling the truth, I suppose we should wait here for Mordred. At least you can't doubt the boy's courage."

"I've never doubted his courage," Terence said. He dropped from his horse and sat in the grass, but Gawain stayed mounted. If they had to ride away in a hurry, it would be easy for Terence to leap into the saddle, but less so for Gawain, in full armor. After about half an hour, the front gates opened and, to their surprise, Mordred reappeared. His face was grim.

"To the king," he snapped. "Quickly!"

"What news?" King Arthur demanded as soon as they were back in the king's council tent.

"He won't surrender, and his position is stronger than it looks," Mordred said solemnly. "Anders has planned this for a long time. The castle is stocked with great mounds of food and enough water for a long siege. But that's not the worst of it. Anders isn't alone. He's expecting reinforcements any day."

Kai swore.

"From where?" asked the king.

Mordred shook his head. "All he would say was that he had friends, some even in your inner circle."

A long silence followed these words. Then the king asked, "And Bedivere? Did you see him?"

Mordred shook his head grimly. "Anders wouldn't let me. But he gave me a message for you."

"What message is that?" replied the king softly.

Mordred looked as if he had just tasted something bitter, and said, "He bids me tell you that if you surrender quietly, he will spare your life."

"Why, that is monstrous kind of him," said the king gently.

Mordred cleared his throat. "He says he will expect your answer by noon."

Arthur nodded. "I believe by then he shall know my answer. Kai, organize lookouts through the night, but tell everyone else to get some rest. We'll be busy tomorrow. And Kai, ask Alexander if he will join me for a moment."

The emperor must have been waiting outside the tent, as indeed was half the encampment, because he appeared at once. "Did you send for me, O king?" Alexander asked.

"How could I *send* for you, my friend? I have no authority over you," Arthur replied. "But I did want to speak to you."

"I am at your service."

"I did not argue with you back in Brittany when you declared your intention of returning with us, but tomorrow we go to war."

Alexander nodded. "Yes?"

"It is not your war, Alexander. You are the king of another land, and we have no official treaties calling for you to join me in battle."

Gradually enlightenment dawned on Alexander's

face, replaced at once by affront. "Is it that you tell me not to fight with you tomorrow?"

"You have your own people to consider. I cannot ask you to risk your —"

"You are very stupid, and you make me angry," interrupted the emperor. "How do your people say it? *Shut up!*" Alexander glanced at Gawain. "That is right, is it not?"

Gawain considered this thoughtfully. "I think you have the expression right. It's not generally directed at the king, however."

"But as he says, he is *not* my king," Alexander replied promptly, looking back at Arthur. "He is my friend. And I will say *shut up* to my friend any time I want, damned it!"

Giving the king a curt nod, Alexander turned abruptly and left the tent. Grinning, Gawain bid his king good night, and he and Terence made their way to their blankets.

Mordred rose from his bed about four hours after midnight, shortly before dawn, and Terence, who had been watching, shadowed him to the perimeter of the camp. There, Mordred tapped a knight on the shoulder and said, "My watch. Get some rest."

The knight nodded and headed back to the camp. Terence relaxed. Mordred was just taking his turn at watch. Nothing suspicious. Then Mordred turned and stared into the darkness where Terence crouched. "Is someone there?" he called softly.

Terence froze, as much from astonishment as caution. He couldn't remember a time when he had been heard in the woods; the silence with which he slipped through even the densest brush was legendary at Camelot. He was sure he had made no noise, but there was Mordred, staring right at him. For a long moment, there was only stillness; then Mordred shrugged and turned away. He walked off, and Terence let him go. *Who is this Mordred?*

About ten minutes later, Mordred returned, humming softly under his breath. He stretched, rubbed his eyes, and gazed again into the darkness where Terence hid. "Hello?" he called gently. This time Terence was sure he couldn't be seen; in Mordred's absence he had moved behind a tree. Once again, Mordred shrugged and moved off, this time in the opposite direction. Mordred evidently had an uncanny sense of other people's presence, which was worth remembering. Terence moved from his tree and slipped beyond the perimeter of the woods, planning to follow Mordred's progress that way, but as soon as he stepped out from among the trees, he caught new sounds: muffled splashings, murmuring voices, the occasional metallic clink of armor. Count Anders's men were crossing the Thames.

Forgetting Mordred, Terence raced back to the king's camp. "To arms!" he shouted. "Attack coming from the river! To arms!"

Moments later the king himself was at his side. Terence told him what he had heard, and the king took over, issuing orders and organizing his men. Alexander appeared, at the head of his Greek knights. "Command me!" Alexander said curtly. "Where do you need me and my men?"

"The party crossing the river before us may not be the only one," Arthur said. "They may have other groups circling behind. Take your men to the rear and watch for ambush."

Even in the dim firelight, the belligerent expression on Alexander's face was clear. He knew he was being given the role least likely to put him and his men in danger. But after a brief struggle, he nodded. "As you wish, Arthur." Turning, he snapped orders in Greek to his men, and they began moving south, away from the river.

Leaving the king, Terence returned to his gear, took up his bow and arrows, and slung them over his shoulder. They would be of little use in the dark, though, where he couldn't tell friend from foe, so he grabbed Gawain's spare sword as well. Then there was a shout, a single clang of arms, and the roar of battle. Terence ran through the dark toward the loudest clamor, and then had no time to think. A dark figure appeared, and a sword chopped down at him. Parry. Parry again. Leap. Thrust. A second figure rushed at him from the other side. Dive. Thrust. Strike. Parry. Then one of the attacking knights jerked and toppled over. The other turned sharply toward his companion and died a second later. A tall knight loomed out of the darkness and jerked his sword from the second knight's helmet, which was now split nearly in two. "Get out of here, Terence," snapped Lancelot's voice. "You have no armor. Go watch our rear."

Terence nodded. Lancelot was right. He was more likely to be in the way in the thick of the fight, at least until the sun rose and he could use his bow. He hurried back through the deserted camp, seeking Alexander's Greek company. A figure flickered to his right, and Terence dropped to the ground, hearing a sword swish through the air over his head. Terence rolled and sprang to his feet, his own sword at the ready. "Squire Terence?" asked a voice. It was Mordred. "Oh, thank God I missed," Mordred gasped. "I saw you running through the dark and I thought the count's men had broken through."

"What are you doing back here?" Terence snapped.

"I heard voices from the rear, that way, and I was afraid someone had circled behind us. Come on! We still might surprise them!"

"Wait!" Terence hissed. "It might be Alexander and his men." Mordred halted, frowning. "Arthur sent them back to watch our rear." It was too dark to be certain, but Mordred seemed momentarily angry. "Let's go quietly together and see," Terence said, adding, "It's good to look before you attack, after all."

He gestured for Mordred to lead the way, which he did, and a moment later they came upon Alexander's men, mounted and lined up, each knight about five yards away from the next, watching the rear. "Emperor Alexander!" Mordred called out loudly, as they approached. "Don't attack. We're Arthur's men!"

"Hush, boy!" Alexander hissed fiercely. "There's someone coming; you'll give us away." But it was too late. A sudden spate of voices from across a dark field made it clear that whoever was there had heard Mordred's shout. Alexander swore, then rapped out a command in Greek, and he and his men broke into a full cavalry charge. Mordred started to run the other way.

"Where are you going?" snapped Terence.

"To get my horse!" he called over his shoulder. "I won't be any help to them on foot!"

That was true, anyway, Terence had to admit. Following Mordred, he raced back to camp to get his own mount. A few minutes later, riding bareback, he kicked his horse into a gallop and charged in Alexander's wake.

The evidence of battle was clear. At least seven huddled bodies lay in the field, but it was too dark to see if any of them were Alexander's men. Terence rode on, past another body, and up to the top of a rise. He could just see the first red line of dawn on the eastern horizon, and below him he heard shouts and the clash of arms. Tossing aside his sword, Terence drew his longbow from his shoulder and fitted an arrow on the string. In a moment, he would be able to see well enough to pick his targets. The fighting beneath him was fierce and constant. He heard several shouts in Greek, which reassured him. One of the voices, he was almost certain, was Alexander's. He itched to ride into the fray but knew he would soon be of more use where he was. He waited. The battle raged on. The light grew. Now he could make out individual forms. Half the combatants were on horseback and half on foot. Bodies lay strewn everywhere. There were at least forty men fighting, which meant that even if every one of Alexander's men was still alive, he was outnumbered. Now Terence could make out a cluster of mounted warriors in Greek armor, fighting together, with discipline. A knight in unfamiliar armor separated from the fray and tried to circle around, behind the Greeks. Terence fired his first arrow, and the knight jerked in the saddle and fell.

For the next few minutes, Terence shot arrow after arrow, as fast as he could. Knights and foot soldiers began dropping. Two knights identified where the hail of arrows was coming from and charged Terence, who calmly dropped both before they had gone a half-dozen steps. His marksmanship with a longbow was as legendary as his skill in the woods. The count's men reeled in confusion, and Alexander gave a ringing shout and pressed his attack. The line fell back and collapsed, and then the count's men turned and fled, with Alexander and his men — only about seven now — in full pursuit. Terence was down to only three arrows, but he kicked his horse into a gallop and followed. A drumming of hooves behind him caught his attention, and he looked over his shoulder. It was Mordred, joining the fray now as well.

Ten minutes later, it was over. The last of the count's men either had surrendered or was lying on the ground. Terence rode up to the emperor. "Well fought, Your Highness!" he exclaimed with feeling. "If Arthur wins this day, he will have you to thank!"

A tall knight approached and removed his visored helm. It was Acoriondes. "Sir, let me take some men back to find our fallen," he begged.

"In time," Alexander said. His eyes were bright and red. "This battle is not finished. These men must have crossed the river around that bend, yes? There must be a boat there."

Acoriondes looked startled. "You want to . . . you want to cross and attack the castle? But we have only six men left."

Alexander grinned wildly. "Change armor!"

Acoriondes blinked. "Change . . . you mean exchange armor with some of the dead?"

"They will let us in the castle gates."

"It's brilliant!" breathed Mordred, who had just ridden up. "Come on! At once!"

Acoriondes met Terence's eyes, then gave a half-smile and a shrug, as if to say, *It might work; if it doesn't, we'll all die.* Terence returned the smile and began looking about for a dead knight about his size.

Knights are not generally very good at putting on their own armor, so it was a good thing that Terence was there. For the next half-hour Terence was very busy, going from man to man and helping with the buckles and latches that were hardest for a knight to reach for himself. Last of all, he also put on a suit of armor. The Greek knights were uncomfortable in the unfamiliar English armor, but they looked the part anyway, except that they all chose to keep their own ornate Greek swords. Mordred kept his own weapons, too, a sword on his left hip and a long thin dagger on his right, but Terence chose a new sword from those scattered about.

Alexander barked a command. It was in Greek, but Terence had no trouble interpreting it: *Let's go!* They started around the bend and, as Alexander had guessed, found a broad, flat ferry with a ferryman waiting on board. Terence realized suddenly that if one of the Greek knights spoke, the ferryman would hear their Greek accents, and so he pushed to the front, whispering, "Let me do the talking," to Acoriondes and Alexander. They nodded.

"They were waiting for us!" Terence said, as gruffly as he could. "This is all we have left. Take us across before they attack again."

The ferryman jumped into action, untying ropes while the knights dismounted and led their horses onto the ferry. "Are they after you already?" the boatman whispered to a passing knight — it was Cligés, Terence remembered from the armor — but Cligés only shrugged and moved on. The ferryman took no notice. He was evidently used to being ignored by knights. They crossed the Thames, then piled out on the other side and remounted. Alexander waved his arm in a silent command, and they started up the banks toward Windsor Castle.

At the closed gate they stopped and waited. "Let us in!" Terence shouted as loudly as he could. A head appeared at the battlements, Count Anders himself. He had sent his knights out to battle but stayed behind. "What news?" the count shouted.

"We've got them on the run!" Terence replied. "But these men are wounded." That much, at least, was convincing. Most of the men's armor had blood on it in somewhere.

"And you brought them back here? Get back to the battle! I don't care if they're hurt! They can all ride!"

So much for appealing to Count Anders's humanity. Terence tried a different approach. "But we thought you'd want to be present at King Arthur's surrender. We came back to escort you to the scene!"

This gambit worked. Count Anders seemed struck by the image of himself receiving Arthur's sword, and after a moment called, "I'll put on some armor. Open the gates!"

The heavy wooden gate swung open, and in a flash Alexander and his men were inside, cutting down Anders's men with precision and fury. Now, in full light, Terence could see that Alexander fought with skill and the passion of a berserker. Cligés, too, was displaying great swordsmanship, and then Terence had no time to watch, because the alarm was raised and all the guards and knights left in the castle were running to the fray. For twenty minutes that seemed like hours Terence had no chance to think, only to react. He was not himself a great swordsman — though Gawain had tried to give him lessons more than once — but his agility and reflexes saved his life repeatedly. And then the battle was over. The last of Count Anders's men were throwing down their weapons, and Count Anders himself — still wearing no armor, knelt trembling before Alexander, begging for mercy.

"That is for Arthur to decide," panted Alexander. Beside him stood Cligés and Acoriondes and two other Greek knights, all that remained of Alexander's company. "But you shall live long enough to explain yourself to him." Alexander lowered his sword and said, "Stand up!"

Still shaking violently, Count Anders climbed to his feet. Then a knight strode from the shadows: Mordred. "How dare you, Count!" Mordred demanded in a hoarse whisper. "You have lied to the king, you lied to me! You have no honor and should be executed at once!" He pressed forward, his face mere inches from Anders's, forcing the count to take several steps backwards, as he continued hissing under his breath at the count.

"But you said . . . but . . ."

"Come, Mordred," said Alexander. "Leave him for the king."

Mordred stopped hissing, nodded, and turned away. As he turned, Anders snatched the long dagger from Mordred's belt and leaped toward Alexander. Mordred's sword flashed like lightning, striking off the count's head, which dropped at the emperor's feet. The count's body crumpled and fell between them, Mordred's dagger still clutched in his lifeless hand.

"Your Highness!" Mordred gasped. "I beg your pardon. I placed your life in peril! In my anger, I didn't even think about the weapon at my side. Forgive me."

"Forgive you?" repeated Alexander. "But you saved my life! I should be thanking you!"

Mordred shook his head. "I am glad I was able to

stop him, but if I had not been so careless, you would never have been in danger."

Then the castle gates, which were still ajar, swung open more widely, and into the courtyard strode a company of knights, with King Arthur himself at their head. He looked fiercely at Alexander, in his unfamiliar armor, and snapped, "Where is your master?"

Alexander removed his helm and lifted his chin. "I have none," he said simply.

Slowly, Arthur smiled and heaved a great sigh. "Alexander," he said simply. "We found your armor and feared the worst. Did you . . . did you do all this?"

Alexander shrugged modestly. "It was nothing."

"And Count Anders?"

Alexander glanced at the body at his feet. "Mordred killed him," he said.

Terence saw Gawain enter the castle behind the king, and removing his borrowed helm, he crossed the courtyard to join him. Gawain raised his visor and gazed at Terence in surprise. "What are you doing in that armor?"

"Later, milord," Terence said. "Let's go find Bedivere."

Leaving Alexander explaining his part in the battle to Arthur, Terence and Gawain made their way to the dungeons. "Bedivere!" Gawain called. There was no answer.

Terence stopped in his tracks. In the furthest cell, a shapeless form lay huddled on the stone floor. "Milord!" he called.

They hurried to the cell and turned the form over. It was Bedivere, and he was dead. "Dried blood on his back, milord," Terence said quietly. "Somebody with a dagger."

6

ATHENS

In the days that followed Count Anders's rebellion, there was great joy at Camelot — and great sorrow. All rejoiced that the revolt had been put down so swiftly and decisively, and of all the heroes of the battle, the most celebrated was the Emperor Alexander, whose daring plan had won the day. But those were also days of mourning. Nearly thirty of Arthur's men had been lost, and no loss was felt more keenly than that of Bedivere, who had been the most widely loved of Arthur's inner circle. Proportionally, Alexander's losses were even greater than Arthur's. Of the Greek knights and squires who had fought, half had been killed outright, and several more lay grievously wounded. Alexander himself had three superficial wounds. The only member of the Greek party who had escaped without a scratch was Acoriondes's smiling squire, Bernard. In gratitude to Alexander, Arthur deeded a plot of land near Camelot to him and declared that it should belong to Alexander and his heirs in perpetuity. There the emperor buried his fallen companions, and for a full fortnight, he and the surviving Greeks left the court to keep vigil over their comrades' graves.

The Battle of Windsor led to another ceremony as well. After all the funerals had been observed, King Arthur assembled the Round Table and — for his part in the battle and especially for saving the life of the Emperor Alexander — made Mordred a knight of the Round Table. Terence watched the ceremony grimly, but said nothing. In the eyes of the court, Mordred was nearly as much a hero as Alexander.

Two days later the Greeks ended their vigil, and Alexander returned to Camelot with those of his companions who were able to walk. The emperor's arrival was met with an impromptu triumph, as townspeople and courtiers lined the streets and cheered. Alexander only shook his head sadly. "Please," he said, when the shouts had subsided enough for him to be heard, "I am glad to have served King Arthur, but I have buried too many friends to be joyful. Forgive me." Leaving the crowds abruptly, he entered the castle to pay his respects to Arthur.

Sarah, who had been standing beside Terence, murmured, "I don't think I have ever liked Alexander as much as I do now," and followed the emperor into the castle.

Almost immediately, Terence sensed that someone else had filled the place beside him. Turning, he looked into the eyes of Acoriondes. "Squire Terence," the solemn counselor said, with a nod.

"Good day, my lord," replied Terence.

"I am glad to have found you so soon upon our return," Acoriondes said. Terence raised his eyebrows, surprised. Acoriondes said, "I wonder if we might talk privately."

Curious, Terence led Acoriondes up the long winding stairs to the top of the north tower, where not only could they be alone but they would hear the echoing steps of anyone following them. "What is it?" Terence asked.

When it came to the point, Acoriondes seemed uncertain how to begin. At last he said, "It has sometimes seemed to me that you are not a great admirer of young Sir Mordred."

Terence fixed his eyes on Acoriondes's face. "Do you know something about Sir Mordred?"

"I *know* nothing," Acoriondes admitted. "But I have questions. In the days of our vigil I have thought much about things I saw that day that do not make sense."

"Like what?"

"Before I speak, is it true that you were the one who gave the alarm before the battle?" Terence nodded.

"How could that be?" Acoriondes asked. "I was standing beside your Sir Kai as he appointed the sentries, and you were not among them."

"I was following Mordred," Terence admitted.

"I wondered if that was it. I have seen how you are never far from him. But why was Sir Mordred out of bed?"

"He was taking his turn on watch."

Acoriondes shook his head. "Sir Kai did not name Sir Mordred a sentry either."

Terence realized at once that Acoriondes was telling the truth. Kai would never have placed Mordred in a position of trust. So why had Mordred relieved the guard?

"And why," Acoriondes continued, "if you were following Mordred, did you hear the count's men approaching while he did not?"

"I do have very keen hearing," Terence explained, but even as he said it he remembered Mordred's uncanny awareness of him in the dark. If Mordred had sensed Terence's presence in utter blackness, why had he not sensed the approach of the enemy?

"Or the other sentries?" Acoriondes went on. "Have you wondered why they heard nothing?" Terence shook his head, but he was beginning to wonder now. Acoriondes's lips set grimly, and he said, "Now I will tell you what I found when I was searching the field after the battle: two men lying between Arthur's camp and the river, with their weapons sheathed and their throats cut."

"You think they were the other guards?" Terence asked, his eyes widening.

"I cannot say. I do not know your knights or remember who were the sentries. But why would anyone have gone into battle with his sword undrawn?"

Terence gazed bleakly from the tower at the bright, sunny pastures below.

"Here is another question," Acoriondes said. "Did not Sir Mordred tell the king that Count Anders was provisioned for a long siege?"

"Yes," Terence said slowly, comprehension dawning. "But he wasn't, was he?" Terence had been among those who, after the battle, had searched the castle. They had been looking for hiding rebels, not supplies, but now he realized that there had been no stores of food. Then he shook his head. "But that doesn't mean Mordred was lying; he may have just been repeating what the count told him."

"True," Acoriondes said. "And there's one more thing: at the last, just before the count stole Mordred's knife and attacked my master, could you hear what Sir Mordred was saying to him?"

Terence shook his head. "Could you?"

"No. Only hissing. But I wonder — when the count

drew Sir Mordred's knife, why did he attack Alexander, several steps away from him, instead of Sir Mordred who stood beside him with a drawn sword?"

Terence swallowed. "That *is* strange — unless the count believed that he was in no danger from Mordred." Terence's heart felt suddenly heavy as other details began to make sense. In Mordred's private diplomatic conferences with Count Anders, had they been seeking terms of peace, or plotting this rebellion together? And when Mordred killed Anders, had he been saving Alexander's life or silencing one who knew too much?

"And yet," Acoriondes said, "all of these questions could be answered without casting the slightest blame on Sir Mordred."

Reluctantly, Terence agreed. Even Mordred's unassigned guard duty could be explained: Terence could just imagine him saying that he had been unable to sleep anyway and so thought he would let some guard have rest before the battle. "So what do you think?"

"I think," Acoriondes said, "that either your Sir Mordred is guiltless, or he is very dangerous indeed. At the imperial court at Constantinople, I am acquainted with many courtiers who live for nothing but intrigue. If Sir Mordred is really behind all this, he surpasses them all."

A week later, Mordred announced his intention to ride out alone in search of adventure. Since this was perfectly normal, even expected, of a new knight, there was nothing in it to arouse misgivings in anyone who wasn't already suspicious. Terence hated the thought of Mordred going off on his own, but after his experience in the dark before the battle, he knew he couldn't follow Mordred unnoticed. He had to stand with the rest of the court and watch him ride away alone.

Over the next week, Terence discovered to his considerable dismay how popular Mordred had made himself among the younger members of the court. The ladies missed him acutely and publicly, sighing over his exquisite taste and continental manners, while the men were almost as bad, speaking fondly of his good humor, quick wit, and generous nature. Agrivaine was especially disconsolate. As Mordred's bosom friend, he had enjoyed a position of prominence that his own surly nature and modest knightly skill could never have earned for him. Arthur said little, but he was obviously pleased at these indications of Mordred's charismatic personality and natural leadership. Terence felt ill.

Relief came a week after Mordred's departure, though, as talk about Mordred's qualities was replaced by more sensational news. Lady Sarah had, at last, accepted Alexander's offer of marriage. This was hailed not only by those who were always excited about weddings, but for diplomatic reasons as well. Since Sarah was Arthur's cousin, this union represented a formal relationship between Britain and one of the greatest powers on earth. Of course, it wasn't a very useful connection, inasmuch as Camelot and Constantinople were too far away from each other to be of much practical assistance in a time of war. "But it's not so far!" Alexander protested. "A month of good riding! And besides, our winter court is in Greece." He glanced at Acoriondes. "Athens is closer to England than Constantinople, is it not?"

"No, Your Highness. It would be about the same," the advisor replied.

Alexander shrugged, grinning. "Oh, well. It was a thought. You'll love Athens, Sarah!"

Even Acoriondes seemed reconciled to his master's choice of bride. "It is not the match I would have chosen," he admitted privately to Terence. "I do not admire this new idea of marrying for love. But I must admit that Lady Sarah is a woman of character and honor, and that must be worth something."

Terence suppressed a smile. Being married — privately, anyway — to his own love, he could not imagine entering into marriage *without* affection, but he didn't argue. "Who would you have had Alexander marry instead?" he asked.

Acoriondes shrugged. "Someone from a land closer to ours, at least," he said. "At the moment, the empire is at peace — else we could never have made this journey — but there are lands beyond our borders that might become enemies. There are the Bulgars to our north, for instance, and the caliphs to our east, who have been reported to be building their armies. Allies against such armies would be useful. Alexander's uncle, Alis, has even suggested an alliance with the Holy Roman Empire, as the barbarians to our northwest choose to call themselves."

The only disappointment, from the court's point of view, was that the wedding would of course take place in Alexander's home, which meant that only a select few from Arthur's court would attend the ceremony itself. Various courtiers and ladies began hinting to the king that they would like to be a part of the wedding delegation. But the question of who would go soon answered itself. Late one afternoon, the lookouts atop the castle gates announced the approach of a rider with two horses. The gates were opened and into the main court galloped Mordred. He was leading a second horse over whose saddle was draped the body of a man wearing the now familiar Greek style of armor.

"Mordred!" exclaimed Arthur. "What is it?"

"Michael!" shouted Alexander, at the same moment.

"I found this man on the road," Mordred explained hurriedly. "He was alive, but barely. His English was poor but he managed to give me his message before he died."

Alexander and Acoriondes were already loosening the bonds that held the body in the saddle. The dead man slid from the saddle, his face frozen in a twisted mask of pain.

"You know him?" Arthur asked.

"He is a courtier from Constantinople, a good man," replied Alexander. "Tell, Mordred! How did he die?"

"He had been set on by bandits," Mordred said. "He escaped them, but with two arrows in his stomach. I removed the arrows and tended the wounds, but it was too late. He died soon after, but not before telling me his errand."

Acoriondes pulled open the dead man's soft, richly embroidered shirt, revealing two wounds just above the man's navel. Terence dropped to his knees beside the body and examined them. They looked insignificant, but Terence had known too many battles and tended too many wounds to be fooled by that. Two arrows in such a place would certainly have killed this man — slowly and painfully, but certainly. Thoughtfully, he fingered the soft material of the man's doublet.

"What errand?" Alexander snapped, his eyes glittering with anger.

"It is not good news, Your Highness," Mordred replied grimly. "He fled by night from Constantinople and came to tell you that your uncle, Alis, has seized your throne and declared himself emperor in your place."

Alexander's eyes flashed, and he turned to King Arthur, declaring, "My friend, I am feared to have to leave your hospital!" Terence guessed that he meant *hospitality;* Alexander's English always suffered when he was excited.

Terence glanced at Acoriondes and read doubt in his eyes but had no chance to inquire further. Arthur said, "Then let us go together. I will muster my own troops and join you. You fought on my behalf when Count Anders rebelled against me. I can do no less for you!"

Stunned, Terence looked sharply at Mordred and saw — or did he imagine it? — a fleeting expression of satisfaction. But Alexander replied promptly. "That you must not, my friend! You have just fought a traitor here, and there may be others. Remember, Count Anders said he had allies. If you leave, you put own kingdom in danger!"

Arthur hesitated, and Mordred stepped forward. "My king, if you choose to repay your debt to Alexander by leading troops against his enemies, I offer myself at your service to watch your kingdom again. I made grave mistakes when you left me in your place before; I will not make those mistakes again."

Terence thought his heart would stop. Surely Arthur would not trust Mordred with England a second time! Then Acoriondes cleared his throat. "Your Highness? May I make a suggestion?" Arthur nodded, and Acoriondes said, "I believe that my master is correct; your place is here. But you could send a troop of your best soldiers, under the command of an experienced warrior — Sir Gawain, let us say." Terence was watching Mordred, who nodded with approval. Then Acoriondes added, "And you should send Sir Mordred with him." Mordred's eyes widened and he opened his mouth to speak, but Acoriondes had already continued. "A young knight of such promise could learn much from a seasoned warrior such as Sir Gawain, and from visiting foreign lands as well."

"It is well said," Arthur replied promptly. "Gawain? Mordred? You will accompany Alexander to Constantinople! Choose your men well! You leave at Alexander's command." Mordred closed his mouth, but when his eyes rested on Acoriondes, their expression was ugly.

Alexander bowed. "This, I accept." Then he turned to Sarah. "My love, our wedding must wait, I am feared. But when I am back on my own throne, I shall return for you."

"And I shall wait," Sarah replied calmly.

"You told me once," Terence commented to Acoriondes, "that at Constantinople you knew many schemers."

"Yes?" Acoriondes replied. They were several days into France, more than a week into their journey, but in the close quarters of a military expedition this was the first opportunity that Terence had found to speak privately with Acoriondes.

Terence said, "I have been thinking that, as far as clever manipulation goes, you probably match them."

The sober Greek's lips quivered, but he only replied innocently, "What do you mean?"

"That business back at Camelot, when Mordred brought your messenger. You turned the tables very neatly on Mordred, didn't you?"

Acoriondes inclined his head, acknowledging the compliment. "Perhaps. I still am not certain that your Sir Mordred is the plotter that we have suspected, but it did seem to me that he was too eager for King Arthur to depart and leave him in charge."

"Did you see the look he gave you when you made your suggestion?"

Acoriondes nodded. "I did. I have asked Bernard to watch my back."

They rode together in silence for a moment, and then Terence said, "I've been wanting to ask you: What do you think of this report from Constantinople? Could Alexander's uncle truly have seized power?"

Acoriondes frowned. "I would not have believed it. Alis is not a man of decision. I would have said he has too little energy or ambition to do such a thing. Indeed, when Alexander appointed him regent, he tried to refuse."

"So, the message was a lie?"

Acoriondes sighed. "I cannot be sure. Alis may have fallen under the influence of others. I can think of many who might use him for their own ends. I wish that Michael, the messenger, had lived longer. But not with such wounds as he had."

"He didn't die of his wounds," Terence said calmly. "Didn't you notice? There was no blood on the messenger's clothes."

Acoriondes blinked, then frowned. "Not die of . . . what do you mean?"

"Wounds like that would have bled freely," Terence explained. "And even if Mordred had cleaned his body when tending the wounds, there would have been blood all over his tunic. But his garment was soft and clean."

Acoriondes frowned. "So . . ."

"So whenever your Michael received those two wounds — whether they were from arrows or a dagger — his heart had already stopped beating."

They had no chance for further speech, because at that moment Dinadan approached. Dinadan had been chosen one of the Camelot party, despite his lack of skill with weapons, because he had traveled extensively on the continent and spoke several languages. "Good afternoon, sir," he called as he drew near. "Hallo, Terence."

"Sir Dinadan," Acoriondes replied with a curt nod. Dinadan, with his irreverent wit, was not one of the Greek's favorites. Terence returned Dinadan's smile.

"You two should be careful, riding off for a tête-à-tête this way," Dinadan said, turning his horse and joining them. "Remember last time we were in France, how many romances got started? You don't want to set tongues wagging."

"We are both men, Sir Dinadan," Acoriondes replied sternly.

"Ah, yes. That makes a difference, doesn't it?" Dinadan replied. "I say, Sir Acoriondes, could I ask you a question?" Acoriondes nodded. "If you had rebelled against Alexander, the way this Alis fellow has —"

"I would never do so."

"Don't pick at straws," Dinadan replied promptly. "I'm asking you to *imagine* for a moment. You Greeks haven't lost your imaginations, have you? Because the old Greeks had just bales of the stuff — Homer and those chaps, I mean — and it'd be a shame if you'd lost it."

"What do you wish to ask?" Acoriondes replied with determined politeness.

"As I say," Dinadan resumed, "*if* you had rebelled against the emperor, would you scatter most of your armies along your borders while you waited for the emperor to come home?"

"Of course not," Acoriondes said disdainfully.

"Because that's what this Alis chap has done," Dinadan said.

"What?" Acoriondes hissed, lowering his voice. "How could you know that?"

"I've just been scouting up ahead, where I came on

some Languedocian merchants. They've just brought a caravan from Constantinople and are swinging through Champagne on their way home to Toulouse. They say your Alis has divided up the armies and sent them off to watch the borders, then packed up and left the capital."

Terence looked closely at Acoriondes, whose eyes were fixed on the road ahead. "And do you believe these merchants?" the Greek asked.

"Oh, yes," Dinadan replied readily. "They're Cathars."

"What are Cathars?" asked Terence.

"A religious group. I spent a winter with them in southern France a year or two back — fine people, with a taste for music. And they don't lie."

Acoriondes's brow furrowed. "Then this might mean that Alis has *not* seized the throne."

Dinadan frowned. "No, that much seems to be true. The Cathar merchants referred to Alis as the new emperor of Rome."

"But that's ridiculous," Terence said. "If you had just seized power, you would never send your armies away."

"No," Acoriondes said. "Neither would you leave the walls of Constantinople, which have never been breached. It sounds more as if Alis were going on vacation — for a peaceful winter at the Athens palace, for

128

instance." He looked keenly at Dinadan. "Did anyone else hear your conversation with these merchants?"

Dinadan nodded. "Mordred was with me," he said. Terence and Acoriondes looked up sharply, and Dinadan grinned at their dismayed faces. "Not that Mordred understood, mind you. We spoke in Provençal, the dialect of Languedoc."

"Did you tell him what you learned?"

Dinadan shook his head. "Haven't told anyone until now." He touched his horse with his heels. "But I thought you'd be interested," he added as he cantered away.

Acoriondes watched him ride off. "Perhaps that fellow isn't as foolish as he seems," he commented. Terence only nodded.

A month later, having pushed their animals for weeks along the Danube River, they turned south into Greece. By this time, Acoriondes's suggestion that Alexander's uncle had moved to the winter palace in Athens had been confirmed by other trading caravans. This news had greatly lightened the spirits of those in the Greek party. Athens, it seemed, was an indefensible city surrounded by ancient walls that were mostly in ruins. With the British knights on their side, and with Alexander at their head, they had no doubt of victory.

As the company neared Athens, Alexander began meeting nightly with Acoriondes and Gawain and Mordred, so as to plan their strategy. Terence was not present at these councils, but Gawain and Acoriondes told him all that was said. Mordred was pushing for a surprise attack, at night; while Acoriondes pleaded instead for diplomacy — asking Alexander to send him and a few men to Alis, to demand surrender. Acoriondes's request was denied, however. Both Alexander and Gawain were, by nature, men of action, and besides, as Acoriondes told Terence wearily after the last council, "No one wants to negotiate with traitors."

"Did you tell them that Alis has sent most of his armies away?"

Acoriondes shook his head. "Our only proof of that is the report from Dinadan's merchants. Sir Dinadan may believe them — indeed I do, myself, though I know not why — but only a fool would base a military campaign on such weak information."

"And so you have been denied permission to meet with Alis?"

Acoriondes nodded, and Terence thought for a long moment. "And what would be your punishment if you disobeyed the emperor?"

Acoriondes looked up at Terence, frowning. "Death, of course."

"Then I'll have to go alone," Terence said. "Is there anyone else in Alis's court who speaks English?"

"You will go across battle lines, on your own, to meet with an enemy? But that's treason."

"I know. How far to the city of Athens from here?"

"Not two hours' steady riding," Acoriondes replied automatically. Then he shook his head. "But you cannot!"

"I can't explain it, but I'm sure that this night attack is wrong. There is something else here that we don't know. I have to go."

"Against direct orders?"

"Are you going to report me?"

Acoriondes was silent.

"When is the attack to begin?"

Acoriondes was still for another moment, then said, "We are to leave two hours after midnight, riding slowly and quietly, so as to arrive just before dawn."

"So I should have a good three hours' lead on them," Terence said.

"More," Acoriondes said. "There are faster ways through the hills for two riders alone."

"Two?" Terence asked.

"I have said many times that I would die for Alexander. That is still true, even if I must die at his own hands. I am coming with you."

Over the next two hours, Terence breathed more than one prayer of thanks for Acoriondes's presence. The Greek countryside was more open than the English forests, allowing the stars and moon to light their path, but in the mountainous maze of crags and narrow passes, Terence would have been hopelessly lost. Indeed, several times he was. Having made his decision, Acoriondes was wasting no time, and more than once Terence lost sight of his guide. Each time, though, just as he was about to give up, he spotted Acoriondes atop some distant hill. The last stretch before the city was comparatively level, and by urging his laboring horse to new efforts, Terence caught up with Acoriondes at the edge of Athens. There were no guards, no gates, hardly a sign of life in all the city. Only a few lights glimmered in windows, and away in the distance Terence saw the placid empty blackness of the night sea.

"Come," Acoriondes said. "The summer palace is on that hill."

They passed through narrow city streets and open areas littered with broken masonry and ancient pillars standing alone, coming shortly to a long palace with no outer walls. Terence, used to high walls and battlements with positions for archers, could hardly believe that this unguarded structure of gleaming white marble was a king's home. Acoriondes banged on the door, which was opened a minute later by a sleepy porter with a lamp. Upon seeing Acoriondes's face, the porter turned white, staggered backwards, nearly dropping his light, and gasped something in Greek. Acoriondes rapped out a sharp command, and the still trembling man threw open the door and hurried away. As they stepped inside, Acoriondes whispered, "He's gone to fetch Alis. He was surprised to see me."

"Really?" Terence replied.

A minute later, a portly man with tousled graying hair, wearing a long white sleeping robe, came running into the entry hall. "Acoriondes!" he called joyously, throwing himself at the counselor's feet and kissing his hand.

For the next several minutes Terence was reduced to the role of observer. Acoriondes raised the man to his feet — this appeared to be Alis himself, and a less imperial figure Terence could hardly imagine — and the two of them spoke rapidly in Greek. Except for the frequent repetition of the name Alexandros, Terence understood nothing of what was said, but from Alis's expressions first of overwhelming joy, then of shock and dismay, Terence surmised that the older man was hearing much that was new to him.

At last Alis set his jaw — and for a moment Terence could see a resemblance between Alexander and his rotund uncle — and called out a command. Acoriondes responded quickly, obviously disagreeing, but the older man shook his head and repeated his command. Then Alis turned and strode away. Acoriondes turned to Terence. "Alis is going back with us, to meet Alexander as he nears the city."

"Will there be fighting?"

Acoriondes shook his head. "Alis is going with us alone." Terence blinked with surprise, and Acoriondes continued, "It seems that several months ago, perhaps six weeks after my master arrived in England, an English messenger appeared at Constantinople bearing word that my master was dead, along with all his companions, killed in a forest fire."

Terence considered this new information. "That's why the doorman who met you looked as if he were seeing a ghost." He frowned. "But no one was sent to Constantinople after the battle with Anders."

"No, my friend, think," Acoriondes said. "Remember how long it takes for a messenger to travel from Camelot to Constantinople. This messenger, whoever he was, had to have been sent weeks before the rebellion even began. Someone in England wanted Alexandros forgotten. After a time of mourning, Alis assumed the throne — with both Alexandros and Cligés dead, Alis is next in line — then sent Michael to recover our bodies and bring them to Athens for burial."

It was too much to process. Who had the English messenger been? Who had sent him? Why? Terence thought first of Mordred, but he couldn't explain why Mordred would want to cut Alexander off from his uncle or why he would have brought the Greek messenger, Michael, back to Camelot.

Acoriondes seemed to be reading his thoughts. "I cannot explain it either. If it is all a plot, it is a deeper one than I have ever known."

At that moment, Alis returned to the room, dressed in unadorned velvet, wearing no armor and carrying no weapon. He barked a quick command, and they went out the front door to find three fresh horses saddled and ready.

Terence could remember no family reunion to compare with what followed. He, Acoriondes, and Alis came upon Alexander and the combined Greek and English forces about an hour from Athens, at the darkest part of the night. Alexander was riding a few yards ahead of the column, and Alis made his way directly to his nephew. Alexander pulled in his horse abruptly, stared, then called a halt. Alis heaved himself from the saddle, then knelt in the road in front of Alexander's horse. "What is this?" Alexander exclaimed in English. Then, with a quick shake of his head, he changed to Greek and dismounted.

Acoriondes moved his horse beside Terence's and, in a quiet voice, translated for the squire. "Alis is explaining about the messenger . . . Alexandros is asking proof of this story . . . Alis says that every member of the court heard the message, Alexandros can ask the translators if he wishes . . . Alexandros is asking who could have sent such a message . . . Alexandros is saying many very vulgar words . . . He is saying what he will do to the man who sent such a lie . . . more things he will do . . . even more things — that one isn't even possible. I think Alexandros has forgotten that he's already had the man's legs eaten off by rats . . . Wait! This is new."

Alis had diffidently interrupted Alexander's tirade, then bowed his head. Acoriondes nodded slowly.

"What is it?"

"Alis says that he is still guilty. Though his crime was the result of a mistake, not a plot, he still assumed a throne that was not his and has committed treason. He asks Alexander to strike him dead now." Then Acoriondes dismounted and knelt beside Alis in the road.

"I, too, am guilty, my lord," the counselor said in English, "with even less excuse. When I left your camp and went ahead of you to Athens, I disobeyed your direct command. I give you my neck as well."

Alexander hesitated. His right hand grasped his sword hilt and drew the blade partway from its sheath, then pushed it back down. "Why did you disobey, my old friend?"

"Because I was sure that Alis was innocent, and I wished to stop a needless war. If my life is the only one lost today, then I shall be well content with my efforts."

Terence wondered if he ought to offer to let Alexander execute him as well, since he had done the same thing as Acoriondes, but on the whole he didn't feel like it, so he held his peace.

Alexander frowned for a moment. At last he spoke. "I will not say that what either of you has done is — how do they say it? — *all right*. You have both deserved death. But I believe that your hearts are loyal, and so I pardon you. It is my right as king to be merciful." Then, having repeated this in Greek for his uncle's sake, he called out in English, "Let us make camp here! The empire is ours again! Who has some good Greek wine?"

Shouts of celebration rang down the line, and knights and squires began dismounting and unloading their packs and building fires and gathering together. Terence looked for Mordred, but in the milling crowds and dark could not tell which figure was his. Alexander embraced Alis, then Acoriondes, and joined in the raucous party that was developing around them. Bread and cheese and figs and salted meats were spread out on blankets — a military feast — while Alexander procured from somewhere a bottle of wine.

"This one is mine!" he declared jovially. "The rest of you have to find your own." He raised the bottle in a toast and called out, "To Lady Sarah of Milrick, soon my empress!" and took a long drink from the bottle. A few seconds later he choked, gasped, tried to speak, then fell to his knees and crumpled over on his side. Frantically shoving three petrified knights to one side, Terence threw himself to the ground beside the emperor, feeling at his neck. Behind him he was vaguely aware of an agonized scream — it sounded like Alexander's brother, Cligés — then heard Acoriondes's pleading voice gasping, "Terence! Terence!"

Terence looked up into his friend's eyes. "He's dead," Terence said.

BOOK II:
CLIGÉS

7

THE ELIXIR OF GOOD DREAMS

Terence had come to Greece to fight a war, and afterward to attend a wedding. He stayed for a friend's funeral.

The Emperor Alexander was laid to rest with great honor and deep grief. It was clear that the people of Greece regarded Alexander in much the same light as the English regarded King Arthur — as that one ruler in a hundred who actually put their welfare above his own — and they mourned his passing accordingly. Since Alexander had no sons, Cligés was declared his successor. He promptly declined the throne — at least until he came of age in two years. At that time, under imperial law, he would have no choice, but until then he was permitted to leave the government in the hands of a regent. He immediately named Alis to continue in that role. Cligés said he could never replace his brother and refused to let people call him emperor; Alis only looked weary at the thought of two more years of rule.

To be sure, there had been some who, shortly after Alexander's death, had wondered if perhaps Cligés had poisoned his brother so as to seize the throne. Several of the Greek courtiers speculated openly on this possibility, showing no particular surprise or outrage at the idea, and Terence began to understand what Acoriondes had meant when he said that the imperial court had a history of plots. But even the Greeks had to admit that Cligés's grief for his brother was genuine and that it would be very odd for him to murder his brother then refuse to take his place. After Cligés, suspicion turned to Alis, who had already assumed the throne once, but in the light of Alis's offer to let Alexander execute him, that theory sounded hollow as well. Terence had his own suspicions, of course, but he still could think of no reason for Mordred to have done such a thing. In the end, no one had seen who gave Alexander the poisoned wine, and that was where the matter rested.

Once the funeral and the period of mourning were over, Gawain began talking about returning to England. Terence knew that Count Anders's rebellion was never far from his mind, and that his friend was eager to be at Arthur's side again. The English troops set a day for their return and began provisioning for the journey. On the night before their departure, as the English knights were meeting with Acoriondes to discuss their route home, they got a surprise. Upon being asked for his opinion on some matter, Mordred said, "Do you know, I think I won't be going with you."

"Eh?" said Gawain.

"You remember what King Arthur said when he sent me with you — that it would be good for me to visit foreign lands?" He frowned thoughtfully. "Or rather, wasn't that helpful suggestion from our dear Greek friend? Oh, well — it doesn't matter. Now that I'm here, I think I might do some traveling, maybe visit the Holy Lands. After all, I was out looking for adventures when all this started, remember?"

Terence had mixed feelings about this. On the one hand, anything that kept Mordred away from England seemed a good thing; on the other hand, anything that kept Mordred out from under his watchful gaze seemed dangerous. At that point, Dinadan's drawling voice interrupted his thoughts. "Since you bring it up," he said, "I've been thinking the same way myself. These Greek musicians have some fascinating instruments, and once I get the hang of the language, I'd like to hear their stories. I might just stay here awhile." He glanced at Acoriondes. "So long as it's all right with the regent, of course."

Acoriondes bowed his head. "I am sure it will be, Sir Dinadan. And if it is not convenient for him, I would be honored to have you as my own guest. Indeed, if I might make so bold, I have another suggestion." He raised his eyes to Terence's and said, "I have been mourning your departure already, my friend, wishing that I could show you more of our lands and customs. Could I persuade you to be my personal guest here at Athens, Squire Terence?"

Terence hesitated for only a second. If Mordred wasn't returning to England, there was no need for him to do so, either.

"Why, yes," Terence said. "I think I would enjoy that. You don't mind, do you, milord?"

"Only if I end up doing my own cooking," Gawain replied.

Later that night, after the council had broken up, Terence led Gawain apart from the others. It was time for Gawain to know all the questions and doubts that he and Acoriondes had had concerning Mordred. He explained it all carefully, and when he had done, Gawain was silent for a long time. "It seems pretty thin," he said at last. "As you say, every one of your suspicions could be explained away by something completely innocent."

"That's why I haven't said anything to you before," Terence replied. "There's not one thing that counts as real proof. But when you have enough little suspicions, they start to add up."

"Maybe," Gawain said. "Or maybe you're seeing things that aren't really there because you're already suspicious. Like this last notion: What could Mordred possibly have to gain by poisoning Alexander?"

"I know," Terence said with a sigh. "But what does he have to gain from any of this? Nothing I can imagine."

"Hmm," Gawain grunted. "Unless he *knows* who his father is."

"What?"

"We've all been taking his word for it that he has no idea which knight it was who fathered him. But if he knew it was Arthur, then he'd know he has a claim to the throne. That'd explain why he might stir up a revolt. If he could bring down the king, then he could step into the chaos and claim the kingdom himself. For that matter, it'd explain why he'd want to keep Arthur from forming an alliance with the empire. It's easier to overthrow a weak kingdom than a stable one. Not that I believe this, mind you, but it would make sense."

Terence pondered this. It did make sense, and it would answer many — if not all — of their questions. Mordred sent a messenger to Constantinople as soon as Alexander arrived in England, telling how all the Greek party had been killed in an accident, so as to put an end to diplomatic relations between the two kingdoms. He didn't want Arthur to have powerful friends. Then, when he encountered the messenger, Michael, and realized that his false message would be revealed, he killed Michael and brought him to Camelot with yet another lie, this time hoping to lure Arthur away from England.

Gawain shook his head. "I see what you're thinking, and you might even make it work, but every new step you take, the more far-fetched it sounds. In the end, do you have any solid reason for thinking ill of Mordred? Something more than the fact that you and Guinglain and Acoriondes don't like him?"

"No."

"It isn't like you to get so carried away by feelings, Terence."

Terence shook his head. "It isn't rational, I know. But it isn't feelings, either. There are other ways of knowing than just through reason."

"None that I'm willing to trust so far," Gawain replied. But then he shrugged. "Still, if you want me to stay with you in Athens, I will."

"No," Terence said at once. "You go back to Arthur. Whatever's going on is bigger than just one person, and Arthur's at the center. Watch over him, and watch your own back, while you're at it."

That was where they left matters, and the next day Mordred rode off alone to the northeast while Gawain led the English party northwest at a good pace, hoping to get around the mountains before the snows. Terence watched until both were out of sight, then made his way back to the palace, where he and Dinadan were sharing a spare room in Acoriondes's official chambers. Dinadan was waiting for him as he arrived, with an expression of irrepressible glee in his eyes. "What?" Terence asked warily.

"I'm so glad I stayed," Dinadan said, chuckling. "I *did* so want to sing at a wedding!"

"What wedding? Who's getting married?" Terence asked.

"The regent, of course: Alis. I shall write a wedding song. Now, let's see, what rhymes with Alis? There's *malice* and *phallus* —"

"What are you talking about? We've been here over two weeks, and he's said nothing about getting married."

"He didn't know it until today," Dinadan replied, shaking with suppressed laughter. "It seems that when he got word that Alexander and Cligés had been killed, he decided it was his duty to marry and have a son — to carry on the family line, you understand. So, he sent a messenger off to the Holy Roman Empire to see if there were any spare unmarried females lying about who might be interested."

"The Holy Roman Empire," Terence repeated. "Yes, that would be a useful alliance."

"Well," Dinadan continued, "there hadn't been a reply, and Alis had nearly given up the notion even before we got here. But this morning, while you were seeing off the others, a diplomatic mission arrived from Germany. They'd gone to Constantinople first, which is why they took so long. Alis's offer has been accepted, and he's scheduled to marry a niece of the Holy Roman Emperor. Wedding plans are already under way."

Terence shrugged. "I don't care for arranged marriages like this myself, but I suppose from a policy standpoint, it makes good sense. What's so funny?"

"Wait until you see Alis," Dinadan replied.

A few hours later, Terence understood Dinadan's amusement. Joining Alis, Cligés, and Acoriondes for a midday meal, Terence could hardly believe the pall that hung over the regent. He seemed, in many ways, worse off than he had been at Alexander's funeral. There he had wept freely and openly, but now he just seemed pathetic and hopeless. He picked at his food, muttered to himself, and sighed repeatedly. "Is something troubling the bridegroom?" Terence whispered to Acoriondes.

"I've just spent the whole morning convincing the regent that, having proposed the match himself, he cannot back out. It would be to insult the German emperor."

"Alis doesn't wish to be married now?"

"He never did," Acoriondes replied. "He still loves his wife, who died two years ago. Alis only proposed the match out of duty, because he had no sons to inherit the throne. But of course now that Cligés has shown up alive, the throne already has an heir. So Alis is betrothed for nothing. To a fifteen-year-old girl."

"Fifteen?"

Acoriondes nodded and added, "Alis's youngest daughter is twenty-three."

Terence winced. Fifteen was not an unusual age for a girl to be married. Guinevere had been scarcely older when she married Arthur, and many girls were wed even younger. But a portly, graying widower with adult children, who was still faithful to the memory of his late wife, could hardly be considered a suitable mate for such a child. Alis looked pleadingly across the table at Cligés and asked a plaintive question, to which the young man replied with a forceful negative.

Acoriondes leaned close to Terence. "The regent asked —"

"I think I got it," Terence said.

A serving girl with a freckled face came in to replenish Alis's wine cup, which he had drained very quickly. Alis glanced up at the girl and asked a question. She gave a two-syllable reply, then giggled in embarrassment. Alis closed his eyes, then began swigging back the wine again. Acoriondes whispered, "The regent asked her age."

"And?"

"She's fifteen."

"Ah," Terence said. Alis was probably imagining being married to that inane giggle. "I can see how he might be depressed at the thought of marrying such a child."

Cligés, across the table, leaned toward them. For the first time since his brother's funeral, a trace of a smile flickered across his face. He spoke in halting English. "If my uncle is depressed, think how the girl will feel to see him."

"You could help them both, you know," Acoriondes replied, "by agreeing to take your uncle's place. It would be in the interest of the empire."

"But no!" Cligés replied at once. "I do not wish to marry a child while I am so young myself. Neither am I seeing why I must save my uncle from his own stupid plan."

It was hard to argue with that, as even Acoriondes seemed to acknowledge. He turned to look at Terence. "My friend, I know that I invited you to stay so that I could show you more of my own lands, but I fear that I shall be traveling north with the regent soon. Do you think that you and Sir Dinadan would be willing to travel with me?"

Terence grinned. "For myself, I stayed to further my friendship with you, so it little matters where we go. As for Dinadan, I don't think he'd miss this wedding for the world."

It was not a wedding that anyone present would forget. Alis and his entourage left Athens two days later, heading toward the city of Mainz, where the wedding was to take place. Messengers flew back and forth between the two courts, so that hardly a day of their journey went by without their getting some new information regarding the upcoming ceremony. They compared notes on the correct colors to wear (purple and gold), on how to celebrate the wedding afterward (a ball and a banquet, followed by a tournament the next day), and even the appropriate proportions of Greek wine and German wine. It was agreed to use the two different wines in equal measure, but as Dinadan pointed out, if Alis didn't ease up on his own visits to the wine wagon, they wouldn't have any Greek wine left to share.

By far the most ticklish issue was religion. It seemed that the eastern branch of the church, based in Constantinople, and the western branch, based in Rome, didn't get along, and so the question of whose priest would perform the ceremony became quite a thorny problem.

"It is all supposed to be about a word in the creed," Acoriondes explained to Terence and Dinadan. "The Roman church uses one extra word."

"What word is that?"

"*Filioque*," Acoriondes replied.

"Oh, right. Of course it would be in Latin," Terence said.

"For shame, Terence," said Dinadan. "You didn't really think that the church would fight over something that people could understand, did you?"

"It means 'and from the Son,'" Acoriondes explained.

"Oh, that helps. Thanks," said Dinadan, his grin growing.

"I think it has to do with the Trinity, and who comes first, and did the Holy Spirit come from . . ." Acoriondes trailed off. "No, that's not it. It's about whether the Spirit *proceeds* from the . . . from the . . . Well, it doesn't really matter. The real issue is something else, anyway."

"What's that?"

"The pope in Rome," Acoriondes said bluntly. "The western Christians call him the Vicar of Christ."

"And what do the eastern Christians call him?" asked Terence.

Acoriondes hesitated. "How to capture the sense of it in English?" he mused. "They call him . . . Yes, I think this will do — I heard a kitchen maid say it in England — they call him 'a knob-headed booberkin.'"

Terence chuckled, and Dinadan asked innocently, "And that's not the same thing as Vicar of Christ, right?"

"That would depend on whom you ask," Acoriondes replied gravely.

"So what will the two empires do?" Terence asked.

"The only thing they *can* do," said Acoriondes. "They have agreed to have two bishops standing side by side, both doing the complete ceremony: one in Greek, one in Latin."

"So we have to do the whole thing twice?" asked

Dinadan. "They can't just take turns and each do different bits?"

Acoriondes shook his head. "The thing is, both churches have declared that the other church is false, so both sides say that a wedding done by the other sort of bishop won't count. The German emperor doesn't care about the doctrinal differences, but he doesn't want to take a chance on the wedding's being declared null. Everyone's finally agreed to this plan, to poor Alis's dismay."

"Yes, I'd noticed he'd perked up a bit lately," Dinadan commented.

Acoriondes nodded. "He thought perhaps they would have to cancel the whole thing because of the religious differences. But the word this morning was that it was settled at last."

"What did Alis do?" asked Terence.

"He said, 'Of all the bloody times for a church to be reasonable!' Then he went to the wine wagon."

The wedding was a colossal spectacle, with the Germans and the Greeks each trying to prove their supremacy by the lavishness of their clothing and gifts. By prior agreement, the bride wore a heavily jeweled veil that completely concealed her face — according to Greek custom — while the groom wore ornate and gilded German armor that, as it happened, was too tall for him, and much too tight around the waist. A team of armorers worked all night before the wedding to make it fit. Another diplomatic crisis loomed when the German emperor, Karl, commented the night before the wedding that the bride would have forty-two ladies-in-waiting. Alis, in response to this news, hastily assembled several extra knights and even a few squires, so that he appeared on the wedding day with forty-three groomsmen. At that point, Karl rushed two more ladies out of the crowd, which Alis countered with one more gentleman, leaving them tied at forty-four. Acoriondes breathed a sigh of relief.

But if the German emperor and the Greek regent were in competition, it was nothing to the two bishops. Both wore gorgeous silken robes, embroidered in gold thread: the Roman bishop wore white and the Greek red. Both carried heavy staffs of gold with the ends encrusted with various jewels, and both wore impossibly high, pointy hats, but the Roman bishop's hat was several inches taller than that of his counterpart. Throughout the morning, the Greek bishop kept glancing resentfully up at the other's headgear. Each carried a large book — Bibles, Terence supposed — bound tightly closed in tooled leather, and a small book containing the actual words of the wedding ceremony. The Roman bishop wore a golden chain around his waist, from which hung a heavy golden key, to which the bishop drew attention periodically by shaking his hips and making the dangling key sway.

"Why does the Roman chap keep twitching his hips? Is it a dance?" Dinadan whispered to Terence.

"I think that key must symbolize something," Terence replied. "Because the other fellow refuses to look at it."

"Judging from where it's hanging, I suppose it means something rude," Dinadan said, nodding. "I wouldn't look at it, either."

The ceremony began, and after a moment Acoriondes joined Terence and Dinadan. He looked exhausted, having spent the past several hours managing all the final arrangements on the Greek end. It was a tribute to his considerable diplomatic skill that he had not only gotten everyone in position in time but managed to avoid being pressed into service as one of the forty-four groomsmen. "I would rather organize a war than a wedding," he muttered.

"I've heard Kai say the same," Terence commented.

"The two things aren't so different, really," mused Dinadan. "Both start out with high hopes and then —"

"You couldn't say that everyone has high hopes," Terence interrupted. "Look at Alis."

The slender bride, covered from head to toe in gold and jewels and damask veils, was making her way down the long aisle, attracting *ooh*s and *aah*s and drawing every eye — but Alis was standing at the head of the church between the two glaring bishops, staring morosely at his feet. He appeared to be drawing a picture in the carpet with his armored toe.

"He's already been at the wine, hasn't he?" asked Dinadan.

Acoriondes nodded. "I think he will not pass out until after the ceremony," he said. "I instructed his man to add water to his cup after the first bottle."

"Ah, young love," Dinadan murmured.

The bride arrived at the altar. One of the groomsmen nudged Alis and turned him around to kneel beside her, facing the prelates, who both began speaking at once. Then they stopped at the same time and glared at each other. "Oh, no!" moaned Acoriondes. "We didn't agree which one would go first! How could I have forgotten that?"

The bishops started again, still in unison, but this time they didn't stop. In fact, they seemed to be speaking faster every second. "It's a race!" Dinadan said gleefully. "My money's on the Roman chap. He looks like he's got staying power, what the horse breeders call 'good bottom.'"

"He certainly has one of those," Terence agreed. "But the Greek bishop's louder."

"Mere flourishing," Dinadan snorted. "He'll run out of wind at this rate. You've got to pace yourself for a long event like a full state wedding. Wait till they come down the stretch."

It seemed that Dinadan was correct, because as the rite went on, the Greek bishop's voice began to crack and to grow fainter. The Roman bishop smiled, as if sensing victory, and sped up. Then, suddenly, the Greek prelate lifted his heavy staff and brought the end down, hard, on the Roman bishop's toe. The Roman bishop squawked, stopped reciting the wedding vows, and began to turn red.

"Foul!" cried Dinadan. "You saw it! A clear foul! Disqualify the Greek!" But the Greek bishop seemed to have gotten his second wind and was doggedly pushing on with the Greek wedding vows. "I shall lodge a complaint with the proper authorities," sniffed Dinadan.

"Wait," Terence said. "Your fellow's down but not out. Watch!" The Roman bishop had begun again and was flipping through the pages of his little pocket missal with great rapidity. "He can't be reading it all. He's skipping parts."

"Nothing in the rules against that," Dinadan said.

"How do you know? You're making this up."

"Look, he's done! The Roman comes from behind and wins!" Sure enough, the Roman bishop had stopped talking and was already fumbling with a golden ring, trying to push it onto the bride's finger. Alis had to all appearances fallen asleep at the altar. The Greek bishop finished off in a rush and, pushing the Roman's hand away, began trying to put his own ring on the girl's hand. The Roman bishop pushed back, using his greater weight to shoulder the Greek aside. With a wave of his hand, the Greek bishop knocked the Roman bishop's tall hat onto the floor behind them. Shocked, the entire company stared for several long seconds at the scene before them. Then the eastern bishop took a deep breath and announced something loudly in Greek.

"What did he say?" Terence asked Acoriondes.

The grave counselor closed his eyes wearily, but he answered, "He suggests that the Roman bishop should shove his *filioque* up his . . . I do not know the English word."

"Liar," said Dinadan. "You know perfectly well —"

"Never mind," Terence said. "We know the word you mean."

Dinadan cocked his head to one side. "Say, what's the Greek word for that, anyway?"

At that moment, Alis woke from his reverie. He stirred, looked blankly around him, and then stared vaguely at the ring on his bride's finger. Terence wasn't sure which bishop's ring it was. Then Alis, as if growing dimly aware of his own responsibilities, bowed his head gallantly to his new bride, who had knelt without moving through the entire ceremony. He lifted the bride's veil to give her a dutiful kiss.

"Dinadan!" hissed Terence. "Isn't that . . . wasn't she at Camelot?"

Dinadan wiped his eyes, still shaking slightly, and followed Terence's gaze. "No, it . . . You're right. It is! That's that empty-headed little chit who never stopped talking all the time she was in England: Fenice."

"That's the name. But I thought she . . ." Terence trailed off. He had a feeling there was a reason Fenice shouldn't be marrying Alis — more than just the age difference — but he couldn't recall what. Acoriondes gestured to the musicians, who launched into a lively recessional march. The Emperor Karl, who had stood behind Fenice through the ceremony, took her hand and placed it on Alis's. Then he nodded to Alis's first attendant, Cligés, indicating that he should help the regent to his feet and down the aisle. Cligés didn't move. He was staring blankly at Fenice's face.

Alis lifted his hand to Cligés, obviously asking for a hand up, and muttered something in the stentorian whisper of the very drunk. Cligés didn't respond.

"Oh, dear," said Dinadan. Emperor Karl snapped something at Cligés in German, but Cligés didn't move. Dinadan whispered, "He wants to know if every Greek is a bleeding sot."

Still Cligés stood motionless, gazing at Fenice's countenance. At last, Fenice looked up. Her eyes met Cligés's, and she promptly fainted.

Alis looked bemusedly at his unconscious wife and asked a question loudly. Terence and Dinadan both glanced at Acoriondes, who at the moment looked very old. "He thinks she's a little young to be so drunk," Acoriondes translated.

The spell broken at last, Cligés thrust his uncle aside and threw himself to his knees beside Fenice. He was murmuring something in Greek to her and rubbing her hands, but nothing made any difference. Then a plump, middle-aged woman from far back in the ranks of the ladies-in-waiting, somewhere between numbers thirty-five and forty, pushed her way to the front. Producing a small bottle from somewhere among the folds of her sleeves, she muttered a few words, poured a drop from the bottle into Fenice's mouth, and touched the bride's forehead. The girl jerked awake. The woman and Cligés each took an arm and helped Fenice up. Then they supported her down the aisle, one on each side. The German emperor rolled his eyes and looked grim, but with the help of three Greek groomsmen, managed to lift the sprawling Alis to his feet and keep him upright and moving until they, too, had left the church. After them followed the two bishops, each holding his jeweled mitre like a quarterstaff and glaring at the other. Finally the rest of the ladies and groomsmen trooped out.

Dinadan sniffed and, in a voice quavering with emotion, said, "Wasn't it beautiful? I just love weddings!"

The wedding was over, but from Acoriondes's perspective it was only the first stage of a grueling ordeal. After the ceremony, which finished in midafternoon, there was a ball until late in the evening, followed by a banquet, and Acoriondes had to keep Alis from offending his new in-laws through it all. Alis stood up with his new bride once for a very brief symbolic first dance, but after that there was no question of the regent actually dancing. Even walking was a challenge. Fortunately, Fenice didn't seem offended. She was clearly delighted to let Cligés represent his uncle on the dance floor.

By extreme vigilance, Acoriondes managed to keep Alis from drinking any more, with the result that after a couple of hours, the regent had sobered up enough to be somewhat awake. Surly and moody, but awake. He began watching Cligés and his new bride and muttering incoherently to himself as they whirled about the dance floor. Acoriondes summoned Terence with a faint jerk of his head, and when Terence approached whispered, "Could you pull Cligés off to one side and ask him to dance with one of the other ladies for a while? It does not make a good appearance for him to devote himself so exclusively to his uncle's bride."

Terence nodded and followed Cligés and Fenice until the music paused, then stepped between them. "Milord Cligés?" he began.

"Yes, Squire Terence?" Cligés replied.

Terence had no chance to say anything else. Fenice squealed loudly and shrieked, "But yes! Squire Terence! I thought that I see you before! You are the squire of Sir Gawain in England, *nein?*"

"English!" cried Cligés, with delight. "You speak English!"

"But yes! I am very well speaking of it!" Fenice replied, her eyes shining. "And you also! I have learned at King Arthur's court."

"And I, too!" Cligés gasped.

"Milord," Terence began. "Sir Acoriondes says —"

"My name you may call Cligés!"

"And I am Fenice!"

"My lady Fenice, may I have the dance next?"

"It would my very heavy pleasure be!"

The music began again, and the pair took their positions. Terence retreated to Acoriondes's side. "I don't think I helped," he admitted. "In fact, I made things worse. When I spoke to Cligés, they discovered that they both speak English, more or less. So now they can talk to each other as they dance."

Alis began muttering darkly under his breath, his eyes never moving from the figure of his nephew. Acoriondes glanced at Terence. "He's saying something about how Cligés had his chance and turned it down and now he'll be bound if he'll let Cligés make him look a fool. It's the wine talking, but I can't entirely blame him."

"Excuse me," said a woman's voice beside them. Terence looked up to see the middle-aged woman who had awakened Fenice from her faint at the wedding.

"Yes?"

"Perhaps I can help," she said. Her English was flawless. She even had a northern accent, similar to Gawain's.

"I beg your pardon, my lady," Acoriondes said. "My name is Acoriondes."

"And I am called Thessala," the lady replied. "I was dear Fenice's nurse when she was a child." Thessala sighed mournfully. "Ah, it seems but yesterday."

"It *was* yesterday," Acoriondes replied drily. "And how exactly did you think to help us?"

"Your master, my dumpling's new husband, seems to be out of sorts. I have a small drink here that might help."

"My master doesn't care for any more to —"

"No, no," Thessala said hurriedly. "It is not a drink like that. It is more of the nature of a family recipe to remove the effects of other drinks."

"I see," Acoriondes said. "Yes, my family has some recipes like that as well. I've never noticed that they work."

Thessala produced a small bottle and a wineglass and poured a swallow of liquid into the glass. "But if you will only try —"

"I think we need not trouble you, my lady," Acoriondes said, bowing politely. But Alis had seen the wineglass. Snapping a few sharp Greek words, he snatched the glass from Thessala's hand and downed it. Immediately his eyes flew open, then closed, and he sagged back into the chair where he sat. "Hold him up, Terence!" Acoriondes snapped, grasping Alis's other arm. For several seconds the two fought to keep the regent from sliding off onto the floor. At last, by main force, they managed to prop the unconscious regent back up on the chair. Terence glanced around; the nurse had disappeared.

"Is he alive?" Terence asked sharply.

Acoriondes was already feeling Alis's pulse. "Yes, it was not poison," he said.

Then Alis opened his eyes, and his lips widened in a relaxed and pleasant smile. He spoke mildly to Acoriondes, as if greeting him, took a deep breath, then gazed limpidly out at the dance floor. Smiling again, he spoke.

"What did he say?" asked Terence.

Acoriondes looked at Alis, then out at the dance floor, then back at Alis before replying. "He said, 'Isn't my wife lovely?'"

It took Terence nearly an hour to find the nurse Thessala among the crowd at the ball and to maneuver himself beside her. When he did, he caught her eye and smiled. "Thank you for your help, Lady Thessala. I believe that the regent feels much better now."

"It was nothing," she replied.

"You speak English very well," Terence said. "Did you visit England with Fenice this past year?"

"No, I stayed here in Mainz."

Terence smiled. "But you *have* been there, surely."

"Many years ago," Thessala admitted.

"Of course," Terence said. "When you studied with Morgan Le Fay."

Thessala's eyes flew open, and she shrank from him. "How did you know that?"

"I didn't until just now," Terence said, no longer smiling. "But you even speak English with Morgan's accent."

"Did Morgan send you? I haven't done anything to her! Tell her I didn't even go to England, just as she told me!"

"I told you: I was guessing," Terence said. "Morgan didn't send me. But if you did study with Morgan, then you are an enchantress."

"No!" Thessala said quickly, her face white. "I mean . . . I didn't actually finish . . ."

Terence looked sternly at the quaking nurse. "Tell me at once: what was that potion you gave Alis, the regent?"

"It . . . it was not dangerous. It's an elixir I discovered myself. There is no harm, and it only lasts a few hours."

"What does it do?"

"It . . . I call it the Elixir of Good Dreams. When you drink it, then you sleep and immediately dream the desire of your heart. Then, when you awake, you believe that your dream is true."

"Good Gog!" Terence gasped.

"I could as well have called it the Elixir of Happiness," Thessala said, a touch of pride creeping into her voice. "I doubt Morgan, with all her *higher standards,* has anything like it. Is it not the most splendid thing you've ever heard of?"

"Good Gog," Terence repeated.

8

THE DUKE OF SAXONY

The ball ended without further incident, and the glittering courtiers proceeded to a vast banquet hall. There, Alis and Fenice were installed at the head table, and the Greeks and Germans were seated at long tables on opposite sides of the room. It seemed rather adversarial to Terence, but he supposed that mingling the two groups would have been useless, since few from either side spoke the other's language. Terence and Dinadan were seated together on the Greek side of the room, but Acoriondes was at the head table, beside Cligés, who was beside Alis.

"Poor old Acoriondes," Dinadan said, grinning at their friend. "I suppose he's acting as a sort of watchdog up there."

Terence nodded abstractedly. He suspected that Acoriondes had arranged to sit where he could catch

Alis when he eventually passed out, but the regent showed no sign of succumbing to his wine. Quite the opposite, he seemed almost lively. He chattered happily to everyone within earshot, regardless of whether that person spoke Greek, and toward his new wife behaved in a markedly affectionate fashion. Fenice, for her part, ignored her new husband, leaning toward him only so as to look around him at Cligés, on the regent's other hand.

"You know something, don't you?" Dinadan asked Terence suddenly.

"Eh? Know something about what?"

"I've been watching you. Alis is up there making a prize ass of himself over this chit that he never wanted to marry to begin with, and you don't even seem surprised. What's going on?" Terence hesitated, but only for a second. He explained what the nurse Thessala had told him about the Elixir of Good Dreams. Dinadan whistled. "I wonder what the old fellow's been dreaming," he said.

"That's puzzling me, too," Terence admitted. "Whatever it was, it's reconciled him to this horrible marriage."

Together, Terence and Dinadan watched Alis as he babbled to Fenice, whose eyes remained locked on Cligés's. Cligés raised a glass of wine in a silent toast to his uncle's bride. Fenice toasted Cligés in response. When their glasses touched, directly over Alis's plate, it was like a caress. Alis smiled joyfully and snatched up his own glass to join their toast, but by the time he was ready, the other two were already drinking, their eyes still fixed on each other.

"And will his dreams reconcile him to that sort of business?" Dinadan murmured.

Terence shook his head. It didn't seem likely.

With the second course, which was some sort of meat boiled in smelly cabbage, the banquet entertainment began. A lone minstrel with a lute appeared, positioned himself in the center of the hall, and bowed to the newlyweds. Terence glanced at Dinadan, expecting to see him sit up with interest, but the knight's eyes showed only weariness. "What is it?" Terence said.

"I know this fellow," Dinadan said. "He's a French *trouvère* named Kyot. He sings the most appalling rot, and the worst of it is that he sings it beautifully."

"What do you mean?"

"You'll see . . . or, maybe you won't. He sings in French. Thank God for that."

The minstrel strummed his lute, then bowed again. He had a singularly graceful bow. *"Mes seigneurs,"* he began, *"et mesdames, je chanterai le lai du* Chevalier à la Charrette."

Terence had enough French to understand most of this, but he leaned toward Dinadan and asked, "He's going to sing about the knight of the *what*? What's a *charrette*?"

"Cart," replied Dinadan.

Kyot got no further for a moment. The Emperor Karl snorted with disgust and called out a surly question to a courtier. ("He wants to know what ass invited a minstrel who doesn't speak either German or Greek," Dinadan translated.) Alis clapped his hands politely, then reached up and took Fenice's hand in his. Fenice looked at it with patent distaste, then smiled across the regent to Cligés. Cligés cleared his throat and spoke in French. *"M'sieu le chanteur,"* he stammered. *"La . . . la fille qui a mariée aujourd'hui . . . ne comprends . . . ne te comprends pas. Parle-toi Anglais?"*

"But yes," Kyot replied. "I can sing in the English as well. It is well, because the song I sing is a song of King Arthur, the Prince of Chivalry, and of the greatest of all his *chevaliers*, the French Lancelot du Lac."

"The knight of the cart?" Terence repeated slowly.

"He speaks English," Dinadan said. "I didn't know that. But what good will that do? No one here understands English, either."

"Except for Cligés and Fenice," Terence said.

"It is a song of the deepest love that man may know for a woman," Kyot said, "for as a man is greater than other men, so is his love greater than the love of others. And there is no love so great as the eternal love of Lancelot for his heart and life — Queen Guinevere!"

Terence culled his memory of Gawain's vocabulary and uttered a few choice words.

170

"This is what I meant by appalling rot," Dinadan whispered. "It's that 'courtly love' rubbish I told you about, which says that pure love can only be found outside of marriage."

For more than an hour, Kyot sang and played and told the story of how Queen Guinevere had been captured by the evil knight Sir Meliagant, then rescued by Sir Lancelot. Having been a part of that rescue himself, along with Gawain, Terence was able to recognize the occasional accurate detail, but for the most part was horrified by the way Kyot twisted the story to his own ends. Gawain, who had nearly died from the wounds he received on that quest, was accorded only a cursory mention, while Sarah — who Terence believed was the true hero of the rescue — did not appear in the tale at all. But worst of all was the minstrel's casual glorification of Lancelot's supposed adulterous affair with the queen, even though Lancelot and Guinevere's brief romance had ended years before. The Emperor Karl, along with most of the company, had given up on the story, which was no more comprehensible to them in English than it would have been in French. Most were devoting themselves to their meals and chatting among themselves. But Cligés and Fenice sat enraptured, listening to every word. Terence found himself wishing for some interruption to put an end to the story.

Terence got his wish. As Kyot was describing a tournament in which Lancelot was permitting every knight to unhorse him so as to prove his love to Guinevere — it was a bit muddled here — the doors of the banquet hall burst open and a tall knight with a graying beard stalked into the room, followed by a company of knights in German armor. Gray Beard shoved Kyot roughly out of his way, sending him sprawling.

"Bravo! Do it again!" murmured Dinadan.

Gray Beard began to speak, in a ringing voice, and the emperor rose haughtily to his feet and replied. For several seconds, they snapped at each other, then lapsed into a tense, glaring silence. Terence looked inquiringly at Dinadan.

"Oh, dear," Dinadan said. "This is awkward."

"Who is that fellow?" Terence whispered.

"That seems to be the Duke of Saxony, quite the big deal in the empire."

Terence had heard that name before but couldn't recall where.

"He wants to know why he wasn't invited to Fenice's wedding," Dinadan explained.

Then Terence remembered. It was something that he had heard Fenice say while she was at Camelot — the reason she was leaving England, in fact. "Because Fenice was already betrothed to him, right?" Terence said.

"That's it," Dinadan agreed. "As I say — awkward."

The Holy Roman Emperor, the most powerful king of the West, was effectively a prisoner in his own castle, held there by the besieging forces of his vassal, the Duke of Saxony. After the brief exchange of words in the banquet hall, the duke had turned and left the court. All had sighed with relief — except, of course, the Greeks, who had no idea what had just taken place — but their relief was short-lived. The duke had spent many weeks preparing for this confrontation, and the court soon discovered that his armies were camped around Mainz, barring every road and blocking all from entering or leaving.

Terence had no trouble piecing together the rest of the story over the course of the next day. The Emperor Karl had arranged for his niece, Fenice, to marry the Duke of Saxony, a very useful internal alliance, but when the offer from Alis had arrived, he had quickly jettisoned this plan in favor of a grandiose dream of joining two empires. He had sent a hasty message to Saxony, saying that he had decided Fenice was too young to marry, then ignored all the duke's ensuing letters. But the duke had heard, of course, about the imperial marriage and had laid very careful plans in response. What exactly the duke hoped to gain, Terence wasn't sure, but for the time being Saxony held the upper hand.

Karl's knights prepared for war, but the emperor decided to try diplomacy first. He and a company of his best knights rode out, taking Fenice with them. Terence watched the parlay from the castle wall, accompanied by Dinadan and Acoriondes.

"Why is he taking Fenice?" Terence asked Dinadan. "Do you know?"

"He says he wants to show the duke her wedding ring," Dinadan replied. "Though what difference he thinks that'll make is beyond me."

"And he thinks the duke will look at a ring, then just apologize and take off?" Terence asked mildly. "I didn't think Karl was such a fool."

"He is not," Acoriondes said calmly.

As they watched, Fenice extended her hand, but the duke didn't even look at it. Instead he raised his arm in a signal. Perhaps two dozen archers rolled from hiding places and began shooting toward the emperor's knights. The knights quickly formed a circle around the emperor, shielding him from harm as they retreated into the protection of the castle. The archers' arrows sailed harmlessly over the knights' heads as they brought the emperor back unharmed.

"If that's the best that German archers can do —" Terence began scornfully, but he never finished his sentence. From farther down the battlements Cligés's voice rose in a long, despairing cry, followed by a single word: "Fenice!" In their haste to save their liege, the emperor's knights had neglected one other detail. Fenice was still in the duke's hands.

"Is it my imagination," Dinadan mused aloud, "or is this Duke of Saxony rather more clever than our friend the Holy Roman Emperor?"

"So it would seem," Acoriondes said thoughtfully. "Whatever he wants, he is playing his hand very skillfully. Now Karl has no choice but to fight. Is this Duke of Saxony so powerful that he could defeat his own emperor?"

They were soon to find out. The Emperor Karl's men now prepared for battle in earnest, scheduling a sortie for the very next day. Alis, who had none of his nephew Alexander's zeal for battle, made a halfhearted offer to lead the Greek knights out at Karl's side, but his offer was firmly declined. "Karl doesn't want to risk Alis being killed," Acoriondes said. "If that happened all this would be for nothing."

"He probably would be, too," Dinadan commented. "Killed, I mean. Have you ever seen such a mooncalf?"

Dinadan was right: Alis was behaving like a lovesick child, moping about and breaking into tears every minute or two. Acoriondes frowned. "Indeed, my lord Dinadan. I cannot account for it. The regent truly seems to have fallen in love with the child Fenice. He told me — but this is ridiculous — that she is just like his deceased wife."

Terence and Dinadan exchanged glances. Was this Alis's "good dream"? That he had married the image of his former love?

The next day dawned, and Terence, who always rose with the sun, watched from the wall as the Emperor

Karl's army mustered in the castle courts. Beyond the walls, the gray light showed activity in Duke of Saxony's camp as well. He wondered how many men would die this day over an irritating fifteen-year-old girl, and he was glad he was out of it. "Terence!" came an urgent whisper.

Terence turned. "Yes?"

It was Acoriondes, hurrying up the stairs. "Cligés isn't in his room," Acoriondes panted. "And a half-dozen of our Greek knights are missing as well."

Terence and the Greek looked at each other for a long moment. "Oh," said Terence.

Wearing hastily donned armor, Acoriondes led Terence and Dinadan around the edge of the battlefield. They were trying to stay out of the fighting itself, but had to remain close enough to see the battle. "What color is Cligés's armor?" Terence asked.

"Today? Who knows?" Acoriondes replied bitterly. "The silly gudgeon travels with several suits of armor, in different styles and colors. It's his hobby."

Terence grinned. Acoriondes's English was becoming more colloquial every day. Few foreigners would have known that in England, *gudgeon* — actually a type of minnow — could also be used to describe a fool.

"What's the Greek word for *gudgeon*?" asked Dinadan curiously.

"*Moron,*" replied Acoriondes shortly.

"That's Greek?" Dinadan exclaimed with delight. "But I've been using that word for years! I can speak Greek! Cligés is a *moron!*"

"Most excellently spoken, Sir Dinadan," said Acoriondes.

The battle, for the most part, was contained in a low area that lay before the castle of Mainz, flanked by the Rhine River and surrounded by low hills. They circled the battleground on the summit of these hills, scanning the scene below them for any sign of Cligés or the other Greek knights.

"And what do we do when we find the *moron?*" asked Dinadan.

"Try to keep him alive," replied Acoriondes. "Whatever else he is, he is my master, heir to the throne of the empire."

"He won't be in the thick of the fighting, you know," Dinadan commented. Terence and Acoriondes glanced back at him inquiringly, and Dinadan explained. "He's not out here to fight the duke. He's trying to rescue the damsel, like Sir Lancelot."

Terence and Acoriondes both nodded. "Of course," Acoriondes said. "So, if we can find Fenice, we'll find Cligés. Let us move farther back from the fighting."

"That'd be my preference anyway," Dinadan said.

An hour later, they found her. Rounding a craggy

ridge, they came upon a small encampment, where six or seven knights stood guard outside a tent. One of those knights, seeing them, stepped forward, drew his sword, and shouted at them in German.

Dinadan stepped in front of Terence and Acoriondes and replied calmly. For several minutes, Dinadan and the knight talked, and at the end of that time, the German replaced his sword and removed his helm, revealing a handsome, youthful face framed with long flaxen hair. He smiled at Terence and Acoriondes.

"This is Captain Boniface," Dinadan said. "He's in charge of the detail. He also writes poetry."

Acoriondes blinked. "He writes poetry?"

"Short lyrics, mostly."

"But is that important?"

Dinadan raised one eyebrow. "To my mind, it's probably the only thing in this whole bleeding fiasco that is."

Terence interposed a gentle question: "And is Fenice in that tent?"

"Oh, yes. But he's seen no sign of Cligés or the others. I asked him if he'd like to let us take her back and put an end to this silly war, and he said he'd love to."

"Really?" asked Terence.

"But he can't," Dinadan said. "The duke's orders were to keep her here, and Boniface took an oath. You understand."

Terence nodded. He wasn't sure that obeying a foolish order was always the right thing to do, but in a world where nothing else made sense, the only thing that one could control was one's own honor. "Is Fenice all right?"

Dinadan blinked. "I didn't ask. Hang on." He directed a question at Boniface, then translated the captain's reply. "She's fine, barring a bit of weepiness. Nothing to worry about."

Now Boniface asked Dinadan something.

"Boniface wants to know if you really are Sir Gawain's squire. I told him you were when I was convincing him that he shouldn't attack us. And if you are, he wants to know if it's true that Gawain once killed a giant and became king of the Isle of Man."

"Not to my knowledge," Terence replied. "And I'd think it would be the sort of thing that would be hard to keep hidden."

Dinadan relayed this response, then listened to Boniface for a couple of minutes. "Pity," he said at last. "It sounds like a spanking good tale. You're sure Gawain didn't slip out and do it sometime when you weren't watching?"

"Look here," Acoriondes said, interrupting this exchange. "Can't we come up with some solution that will free Fenice, stop this fighting, keep Cligés from harm, and preserve the captain's honor?"

"Is that all?" asked Dinadan. "Almost seems too simple to bother with, don't you think?"

"Many problems are less difficult than they appear," Acoriondes replied. "Could you ask the captain what his master really wants? Surely he did not go to war for the sake of this silly Fenice."

"I'll ask him," replied Dinadan.

He spoke to Boniface, who snorted and rolled his eyes at the tent behind him. *Für die Schwachsinneger? Nein!*

"He says, 'For the *Schwachsinneger*? No!'"

Terence grinned. "I take it that *Schwachsinneger* means —"

"Gudgeon," Dinadan explained, nodding. "*Moron,* if you will."

"Then why?" pursued Acoriondes.

Dinadan asked Boniface. A minute later he explained, "Boniface isn't sure. He suspects that it's all about some disputed lands, though. There are some regions that the emperor and the duke both claim, and the duke is using the emperor's broken promise to seize an advantage in the dispute."

Terence wasn't sure what capturing Fenice had to do with a land dispute, but the Greek nodded at once. "Yes, that makes perfect sense. This battle is simply a prelude to a treaty that has already been worked out."

Dinadan shook his head. "If they've already worked it out, why do they have to fight first?"

"To keep up the illusion," Acoriondes explained.

"They pretend that they care about honor, not merely land, and so they must fight. It is for appearances."

"For appearances," Dinadan repeated. "Now, there's a lovely thing to die for."

Dinadan got no further. At that moment, from a crevice in the jagged and broken rock wall behind the tent, came an attack. Terence saw seven knights on horseback, already riding down the German guards who stood before the tent. He had just enough time to see that they wore Greek armor before he was roughly pushed to one side by Acoriondes, who had drawn his own sword and placed himself between the attack and his English friends. Terence quickly strung his bow and fitted an arrow to the string but then hesitated. Who was he to shoot? The German guards obeying their orders or the Greek knights trying to rescue Fenice from abductors? Captain Boniface drew his sword and raced back to help his men, where he was faced by a knight in shining golden armor. They engaged each other briefly, but the golden knight fought furiously and brilliantly — and had the advantage of being mounted — and within seconds the German captain had fallen. A moment later, the clearing was still. Two Greeks and all the German guards lay sprawled before the tent. The golden knight drew off his helm, revealing himself as Cligés, then leaped from his horse. Tearing open the tent, he strode inside.

For a moment there was silence, then Cligés reappeared, Fenice in his arms. "I have come for you, my lady!" he cried.

"My Lancelot! I have been you expecting!"

Cligés threw Fenice onto his saddle then climbed up behind her while the other Greeks gathered the bodies of their fallen companions. Then Cligés waved cheerfully to Acoriondes, called out something to him in Greek, and led his men away.

"He thanks us," Acoriondes said woodenly. "He had been in the rocks, watching for their chance, and when he saw us distract the captain, he knew the time had come."

Terence closed his eyes wearily. Dinadan walked slowly forward, then knelt beside Captain Boniface. The young knight lay on his side, his fair hair covering his face. Dinadan rolled him onto his back and smoothed away the long hair, revealing open and sightless eyes.

Dinadan's shoulders hunched, as if he had been struck on the back, then began to shake. "For appearances," he whispered brokenly between sobs.

9

THE TOURNAMENT OF PEACE

The battle ended inconclusively that day. Those of the duke's men who had survived the fighting returned to their siege camp, while those left of the emperor's knights went back within the castle walls. But just as the gates were about to close, Cligés and his men rode over a hill, silhouetted by the setting sun, triumphantly bearing their prize — the rescued Fenice. Cligés had obviously timed his arrival for dramatic effect: Terence, Dinadan, and Acoriondes had been on foot and had still arrived back at Mainz hours before Cligés and his men.

The effect was all Cligés could have asked for. The knights of Mainz cheered enthusiastically at Fenice's rescue and acclaimed her deliverer as a hero. Only Emperor Karl and one or two of his advisors seemed unimpressed. Indeed, Karl seemed almost angry. Terence commented on this to Acoriondes, who looked surprised. "Of course he is angry," he said. "All his plans have been overset."

"He's not pleased that his niece has been rescued from abductors?"

Acoriondes shook his head slowly. "You poor innocent," he said at last. "Have you *no* experience with diplomatic negotiations?"

"Not enough, I gather," Terence replied. "Why don't you explain to me why Karl should be disappointed at his niece's rescue."

"Rescue? She was never in danger."

"Never in . . . then why . . . ?"

"Didn't you hear what young Captain Boniface said? This is not about Princess Fenice, but about some disputed territory."

"Yes, of course. But —"

"Look, sometime during the night, two nights ago, just after the duke had laid down his challenge, the duke and the emperor sent emissaries back and forth and made a deal. The duke would resign all claim to the hand of Fenice, and in return, the emperor would give him rights over that plot of land he wants."

"You know this?" Terence demanded.

"I didn't see it happen, but yes, I know it. But it is not knightly to barter women for land. Both must be won by deeds of honor. So, the abduction was arranged to give each a pretext for battle."

"The abduction was . . . ?" Terence gasped, floundering.

"Arranged. Remember, you yourself wondered why the emperor took Fenice with him to the parlay."

Terence blinked, then added thoughtfully, "And that's why none of the duke's archers could hit anything."

"Exactly. They were taking care not to harm the emperor. That would have ruined the plan. Then they went to war. I'm not sure exactly how the battle was supposed to end: perhaps the emperor was to take the duke captive, then trade him for Fenice."

"But how would that — ?"

"In gratitude for the emperor's sparing his life, the duke would then give up his claim to Fenice and vow eternal fealty to Karl."

"And in return," Terence said slowly, "the emperor gives the duke those disputed lands. He would look magnanimous, instead of greedy and conniving."

"And the duke would look like a man who had fought for honor and love, then accepted defeat with grace and courage."

"Quite a touching story, really," Terence reflected.

"Which our Cligés has now made a complete muddle of," Acoriondes said. "And that, my friend, is why

Karl is unhappy. All that complicated diplomacy has been wasted, and they have to construct a new fiction."

"I wonder how many men will die for this next one," Terence said.

It didn't take long to learn what the next story would be. The battle was suspended the next day while ambassadors scuttled back and forth between the camps. At the end of the day, Karl called all his court together for an announcement. Terence and Acoriondes stood on either side of Dinadan as the emperor made his speech.

"He says," Dinadan translated, "that the Duke of Saxony has shown great honor and courage and worthiness and . . . Look here, do you need me to translate all this rot?"

"No, just give us the gist," Terence said.

"Yes, well, it seems that the Duke of Saxony is the perfect knight. Practically a god."

"The emperor must have gotten what he wanted," Acoriondes commented.

"Wait, he's started on something new," Dinadan said, listening. "He says that the duke recognizes the sovereign power and great mercy of the Holy Roman Emperor, who is kind and forgiving and likes small children and puppies and butterflies —"

"He didn't either say that," Terence protested.

"You said to give you the gist, didn't you? The emperor's a saint. Oh, here's the point. The duke recognizes the emperor's right to marry his niece to whomever he chooses, and he freely surrenders his claim to the hand of the Princess Fenice."

"That's it? Nothing in return for the duke?" Terence asked.

"Wait," Acoriondes said calmly. "There will be more."

The emperor began again. Dinadan said, "The emperor accepts the duke's fealty and chooses to forgive all past disloyalties, because the emperor is kind and gracious and puppy-loving . . . Hang on — what's this?" Dinadan listened closely for a minute, then grinned and said, "To honor his loyal vassal, the Duke of Saxony, the emperor declares that two days from now he shall hold a tournament, with all the great knights of Saxony invited to participate. And the winner of the tournament will be granted, by the emperor's great largesse, a fiefdom in the district of Gotha."

"What did I say?" Acoriondes said, smiling.

"Ah," Terence said. "So the duke humbles himself today, and in return, tomorrow he gets to win a tournament and be awarded the lands he wants."

"Quite a clever solution," Acoriondes said, nodding approvingly. "All they have to do now is arrange the tournament so that the duke will win."

"And in the meantime," Dinadan added, still translating, "the emperor knows that his Greek guests have long been eager to return to their homes, so tonight he will hold a farewell feast in our honor. Isn't that nice of the chap?"

"He wants us out of the way before the tournament," Acoriondes said. "You can't blame him, either. After all, it was Cligés who made such a bumblebroth of the last plan."

"Bumblebroth?" repeated Terence and Dinadan together.

"I heard the word from a groom in Camelot," Acoriondes admitted, grinning slightly. "Did I not use it correctly?"

"No, it was perfect," Terence said. "It just sounded odd coming from you."

"What *is* a bumblebroth, anyway?" Acoriondes asked.

"I haven't a clue," Terence said.

"It doesn't mean anything vulgar, does it?"

"Oh, I do hope so," Dinadan said. "Let me think about it on our way back to Athens."

As it happened, though, the Greek party did not leave for Athens the next morning as planned. Shortly after Terence awoke, a grim Acoriondes informed him that Cligés was taken ill and could not be moved. "Ill? How ill? In what way?"

"Fever, delirium. I've just been with him. He's bad,

all right. Emperor Karl's furious about our delay, but he's sent for his own doctors."

Terence frowned for a long second. "Acoriondes —" he began.

"If you're wondering about poison," Acoriondes said shortly, "you are not alone. But who? And why?"

"Well," Terence said, "Karl wasn't happy with him after the rescue."

"Karl's no fool. Having done all this for the sake of an alliance with Constantinople, he wouldn't jeopardize it for a petty revenge."

"Then what about . . ." Terence hesitated.

"Yes?"

"Forgive me, but what about Alis? He believes that he's in love with Fenice, but Fenice is obviously infatuated with Cligés. People have done mad things for love."

Acoriondes shook his head. "I admit that I wondered the same thing," he said at last. "But wait until you see Alis."

"What is it?"

"Come and see."

Terence followed Acoriondes to the private dining room where the Greek royal party ate their breakfast. Alis and Fenice were seated together, along with a few other Greek nobles and Dinadan. Alis looked up anxiously as Acoriondes entered, and earnestly asked something.

Acoriondes replied calmly, shaking his head. Terence guessed he was telling the regent that Cligés had not improved.

Alis bit his lip, then put his left arm around Fenice's shoulders and grasped her right hand, murmuring something gently to her. Fenice took a small bite of sweet bread and accorded him a perfunctory smile. Alis gave the unresponsive girl a squeeze, then released her. She took another bite and edged slightly away from her husband. She didn't seem especially worried, Terence noted.

Alis demanded something else, and Acoriondes replied. Then he translated for Terence. "The regent asks if the doctors have arrived yet."

"Doctors?" Fenice asked, looking up.

"Your uncle has sent for his own doctors, my lady," Acoriondes explained.

"Oh, I should to him also send Thessala! No one knows more about healing than she knows!" Fenice exclaimed. "I must go at once!" Fenice leaped up from her chair just in time to escape another affectionate embrace from the regent. She hurried from the room.

Smiling foolishly, Alis watched her leave. Acoriondes muttered to Terence. "Was that just an excuse to get away from her husband, or do you think this nurse really knows anything about medicine?"

Terence met Dinadan's eyes and saw his own

speculation reflected in them. "It may be that Thessala knows more about Cligés's illness than anyone," he replied. "Let's go see."

Before they could leave, though, the regent launched into a long monologue, and they were obliged to stand and wait until he finished. Terence understood none of what Alis said, of course, but it clearly made everyone else in the room very uncomfortable. Acoriondes's face reverted to diplomatic inscrutability, and his eyes stared fixedly at the wall behind the regent, while the other Greek nobles in the room either turned red or looked frankly nauseated. At last Alis concluded his speech, uttered a deep sigh, and lapsed into a meditative silence. Acoriondes spoke abruptly and turned to leave with Terence. Dinadan leaped up from his chair and joined them.

"What was that all about?" asked Terence.

Acoriondes looked grim. "He was describing how he loves his wife," he said at last.

Terence was going to leave it at that, but Dinadan said, "Rot! You looked like a stuffed frog in there, and the other chaps were thinking about throwing themselves out the window. He wasn't just being gushy. What was he *really* saying?"

Acoriondes scowled. "He spoke of how warm his darling Fenice was, and how she had cuddled him — that is the right word, yes? *Cuddled?*"

"I hope not," muttered Dinadan.

"— how she had cuddled him every night since their wedding," Acoriondes continued.

In a subdued voice Dinadan said, "Sorry I asked. You know, maybe I don't want to learn Greek after all."

They walked together down the hall for a moment, then Terence asked, "Forgive me, Acoriondes, but did he really say *every* night since his wedding?"

Acoriondes shuddered and said, "Yes." Then he stopped in his tracks and looked curiously at Terence. "But that is impossible, is it not? One night she was the duke's prisoner."

"That's what I was thinking," Terence agreed. "But maybe it was just a figure of speech."

A moment later they came to Cligés's room. Entering, they found themselves in the midst of a shrill argument. Fenice's nurse was standing between Cligés in his bed and three distinguished-looking men in long robes and gray beards. After a minute, Dinadan whispered to the others, "The old biddy won't let the doctors bleed him."

The sides didn't seem fair — three official medical experts against one retired nursemaid — but in the end, to Terence's surprise, the doctors backed down and left. Terence wondered if the doctors knew about Thessala's former training in sorcery. Thessala looked up at Acoriondes, Dinadan, and Terence and smiled reassuringly. "You need not worry. All those doctors think about is bloodletting, but really what this dear boy needs is tender care. I will see to him myself."

"My good woman," Acoriondes said, "if my young master dies because you've driven the doctors away —"

"Dies? It will be no such thing, I assure you. You just trust Thessala, and I'll make it all better." She smiled brightly, and Terence had a sense he had just been dismissed. A moment later he and his friends were out in the hall.

"Do the rest of you also feel five years old?" Dinadan asked plaintively.

With Cligés in a high fever, there was no question of the Greek party leaving Mainz, and as the scheduled tournament approached, the Emperor Karl began to show increasing frustration, at least until Acoriondes set his mind at rest. Taking Dinadan along as interpreter, Acoriondes apologized profusely to the emperor for being such a nuisance, then asked the emperor not to expect any of the Greek knights to take part in the tournament. "For none of us," Acoriondes explained, "would feel at all able to join in while our master lies ill."

Relieved, the emperor almost smiled. Dinadan even heard him comment graciously to one of his courtiers that, so long as the Greeks didn't ruin the tournament, he wouldn't even mind if Cligés lived.

The day of the tournament arrived. Alis was to watch the tournament from Karl's own box, but following Acoriondes's strict instructions, none of the rest of the Greeks even went to the tournament grounds. Terence and Dinadan strolled down alone. "Cligés any better today?" Dinadan asked as they walked.

"Thessala thinks so. He's sleeping better, anyway, she says." Thessala had established herself as the dictator of the sickroom, deciding who could enter and for how long. "She wouldn't let anyone in to disturb him this morning, not even Alis and Fenice."

They arrived at the stands that encircled the tournament grounds. Like most such structures, they had been hastily thrown together and seemed on the verge of collapsing, but the nearer one got to the imperial box, the sturdier they were, and Dinadan and Terence managed to find seats that not only seemed stable but also provided a view of the emperor and his guests. Between Alis and the emperor sat Fenice, clearly enjoying the festivities hugely. "She doesn't seem concerned about Cligés, does she?" asked Dinadan.

"She never has," Terence replied.

The tournament began with a mock battle, in which twenty knights of Saxony were pitted against the same number of the emperor's knights. Terence and Dinadan watched closely, not so much to see who would win — they assumed that the Saxons would do that — but rather to see how well they managed to stage that victory. "There," Terence whispered to Dinadan. "See that tall knight with the red shield? He had a chance to unhorse the duke just now."

"I didn't see anything," Dinadan said. Terence grinned without answering, and Dinadan shrugged. "All right, so I probably wouldn't. I never pretended to know anything about fighting."

"No, that's probably why I like you," Terence said. "You don't pretend anything."

The Duke of Saxony spurred his mount forward and unhorsed two knights with one lunge of his lance, prompting a roar of approval from the crowd. "I don't think he even touched that second knight," Terence said, shaking his head. "This is getting a bit thick."

"Was that fellow here when we started?" Dinadan asked, gesturing toward a knight in black armor at the far end of the tournament field, by the gate.

"I don't think so," Terence replied.

The new knight urged his mount into a run and plunged into the thickest part of the fighting, sending two Saxon knights to the ground at once and forcing several others to flee. The crowd cheered, and several of the imperial knights raised their lances in salute. But the black knight only lowered his own lance and charged the knights of the emperor's party.

"He doesn't seem to know what side he's on," Dinadan said.

"Or care," Terence said. "That armor isn't German armor."

"You think it's one of Alis's knights?" Dinadan asked, alarmed.

"It isn't Greek, either. I'd say it was English, myself."

The black knight threw himself into another charge, then another. Wherever he went, knights went down, from both sides. Terence's eyes narrowed. He had spent most of his life around the greatest knights in the world and had learned to identify a fighter's style. He had seen someone who sat his horse like this. "I think I know who this is," he said.

"Cligés," Dinadan replied.

Terence looked at his friend with surprise. "You could see that, too? From the way he sits his saddle?"

Dinadan shook his head and gestured at the imperial box, where Fenice was standing and gazing rapturously at the black knight.

"Ah," Terence said. "She knew he'd be here. That's why she wasn't worried."

"But he really was sick," Dinadan said. "I was in his room just yesterday with old Acoriondes, and he was truly feverish. You can't fake a cold sweat."

"I wonder," Terence said, "if there are potions that

a fellow could take that would make you feverish for a time."

"Thessala?" Dinadan asked. Terence nodded, and Dinadan sighed, "I hate enchantresses, you know that?"

"Not usually my mug of ale, either."

"He took sick the morning after the tournament was announced," Dinadan said slowly. "So if this whole thing was planned, it must have been so that he could enter the tournament anonymously."

"Like in a story of courtly love," added Terence.

Dinadan scowled. "See? That's what happens when stupid people tell stupid stories. Stupider people believe them."

The battle was nearly over. Only the black knight and three Saxon knights were left in their saddles — the duke and two others. The black knight charged recklessly, sending shields and lances flying. There was a minute of furious fighting, but when it was over, the duke and his knights lay on their backs in the mud. The black knight rode over to the imperial box, bowed toward Fenice and Alis without speaking, then trotted majestically away. The Emperor Karl rose to his feet and began shouting over the cheering crowd.

"What's he saying?" Terence demanded.

"Hang on," replied Dinadan, listening. At last he spoke. "He's trying to make the most of a bad thing.

He says that since the unknown knight was of neither camp, he awards the prize for the mock battle to the Saxons and the individual prize for the battle to the duke himself."

Terence was dubious. "Will it be enough for the duke? He's probably in a fury."

"It'll depend on the individual jousting," Dinadan said, considering the question. "That's where the real winner's chosen. If the duke wins that, it should smooth things over."

"But what if Cligés comes back?"

"Karl's thought of that," Dinadan said. "While they set up the tilting yard for the jousting, he's sending his men out to find and, ah, *restrain* the black knight."

The black knight did not reappear, and when the individual jousting began after noon, all seemed to be going as arranged. The individual contests were well fought and evenly matched, except when someone faced the Duke of Saxony. In those jousts, the duke always won easily, moving steadily up the chart toward his inevitable victory. At last, about four hours after noon, there were only four knights left in the contest. The duke dispatched his opponent quickly, if not very convincingly, and trotted over to one side to await the joust that was to determine who would face him in the final test. The two knights took their positions and waited. One was a Saxon knight in brilliantly shined bronze-colored armor who had won every previous joust quickly and decisively; the other was a knight in shabby red armor who had seemed all day to be on the verge of elimination but had always come out on top by the barest of margins, unhorsing his various opponents on the third or fourth pass, with what usually seemed to be a lucky blow.

"Which side is this red chap from, anyway?" Dinadan asked.

"I don't know," Terence replied. "Which side did he fight for during the mock battle?"

Dinadan puzzled over this for a moment. "I don't remember any red knights this morning."

Terence frowned. Certainly not every knight had partaken in the mock battle, but the most skilled knights always did. It would be very odd for a knight who was able to reach this stage in the individual jousting not to have done so. But Dinadan was right. There had been no red knight in the battle. "Maybe he changed armor," he said.

As soon as he said this, he and Dinadan looked at each other with horror. "No!" Dinadan said. Then he turned his eyes toward Fenice in the emperor's box and uttered a muffled oath. Fenice was waving a silk scarf in the air toward the red knight. Red nodded his head in silent acknowledgment of her greeting, then settled himself into the saddle with grim purpose.

Most of the afternoon, the red knight had seemed almost lackadaisical in his approach to his jousts, but now that careless attitude was completely lacking.

"We should have thought of this," Terence said. "Acoriondes *told* us that Cligés always traveled with several different suits of armor."

"I wonder how many soldiers are still out there looking for a black knight," Dinadan mused.

The horn signaled the charge, and the two knights raced toward each other, lances leveled. There was a tremendous crash and both horses reared on their hind legs, but it was the bronze Saxon who tumbled from his saddle. The red knight saluted the emperor's box, then trotted back to his starting position for the final joust.

"Dinadan," Terence hissed, "go tell the emperor that he mustn't let this joust go on."

"What, trot up and tell him that I know he and the duke have been cheating? No, thank you."

"No, you can't do that," Terence admitted. "But you could say that you think that red knight's an imposter. Then he'd realize his plan's in danger."

Dinadan nodded and hurried away. Terence watched as he climbed into the box and made his way to the emperor. A guard tried to stop him, but Dinadan called out to Karl, who permitted him to approach. Dinadan whispered something in the ear of the emperor, who blanched and stood abruptly to his feet. Waving his arms, he began shouting over the cheering crowd. The Duke of Saxony rode near to hear what the emperor was saying, but he didn't respond as Terence had expected. Instead, he shouted angrily at the emperor and rode to his own starting post. The emperor sank back into his chair and covered his eyes with his hands.

The trumpet was sounding the call to readiness when Dinadan returned to Terence. "What was all that?"

"Karl tried to call off the tournament, saying that both of the last two knights deserved a prize and that there was no need for the last joust."

"That was the best he could think of?"

"Evidently. And the duke took it to mean that Karl was trying to back out of the deal at the end."

The trumpet sounded the charge, and a moment later it was over. The Duke of Saxony lay prone in the mud, having flown a good ten feet backwards after leaving the saddle. The red knight was clearly and undeniably the winner of the tournament.

In front of all the court, Karl had no choice but to stand and award the prize to the red knight. He gave a brief, sullen speech, then produced a roll of parchment and handed it to the winner.

"That's the decree granting a fiefdom to the winner," Dinadan explained. "I wonder what Cligés will do with lands in Gotha. Build a vacation home, maybe? Now Karl's asking for the red knight's name. Pity Cligés doesn't speak German."

There was a hush as people stopped whispering amongst themselves to listen. Evidently Terence and Dinadan hadn't been the only ones speculating on the red knight's identity. But the red knight only took the roll of parchment and walked his horse a few steps to the emperor's right, until he was in front of Alis and Fenice. Then, with a courtly bow, he extended the deed toward them. Fenice sighed deeply and placed her hands on her heart, and while she was posing in this affecting attitude, Alis dazedly took the deed. He stared at it for a moment. Then as if it were red hot, handed it quickly back to the emperor.

"None of this was supposed to happen, right?" Dinadan asked.

"I don't think so," Terence said. "But I got lost a while back."

"And what does the emperor do now?"

"No idea," Terence replied. "We need Acoriondes to explain it to us. I'm no good at intrigue."

"That's probably why I like you," commented Dinadan.

"All I know for certain is that Cligés has played hob with another one of the emperor's plans, and poor hapless Alis is caught in the middle."

At this moment, the Duke of Saxony, supported by two of his knights, limped over to the imperial box, his face white with rage, and began a furious tirade. Dinadan listened briefly, then said, "He's accusing Karl of having planned all this."

The emperor turned red, then replied with equal anger, and the two men screamed at each other for several minutes while their knights and entire courts listened in speechless horror. The red knight who had caused all the furor quietly trotted away and disappeared.

"Cligés is gone," Terence whispered. "We'd better go, too."

"So soon?" asked Dinadan. "But I'm learning some splendid new German words. You wouldn't think that emperors and dukes would know such language, but really their vocabulary is quite —"

"Now," Terence said firmly, taking Dinadan by the arm and leading him away.

It was the second evening after the tournament, and the Greek party's second night on the road. Once Terence and Dinadan had explained to Acoriondes what had transpired at the tournament, the sage counselor had sprung into action, ordering the entire Greek contingent to be ready to leave within the hour. And, true to his word, the Greeks left an hour later. Anything that wasn't packed by that time was simply left behind. A few of the Greek knights expressed worry about leaving with Cligés still so ill, but then to their surprise and gratification Cligés appeared himself looking not only completely well but cheerful and pleased with himself. They traveled nearly all the first night, rested for a few hours, then set out again, continuing all day, until an hour after dark. Only then did Acoriondes allow the caravan to stop and the exhausted Greeks to eat a weary supper and go to sleep.

Terence and Dinadan ate at the regent's fire, with Acoriondes, Cligés, Fenice, and the nurse, Thessala, who evidently came with Fenice. Everyone was too tired to speak, except for Alis, who cooed affectionate blandishments toward his indifferent bride. Neither Terence nor Dinadan asked Acoriondes for a translation. At last, after eating, Alis rose and with a besotted smile indicated to Fenice that it was time for them to return to their wagon. Fenice glanced at Thessala, who leaped to her feet and bustled away, returning a moment later with a small glass holding a finger or two of liquid in it, which she presented to Alis. Then the regent and his bride walked away. Acoriondes wore what Dinadan called his "stuffed frog" expression, but Terence noticed that Cligés didn't seem jealous at all. If anything, he looked amused.

Thessala tottered away toward her own wagon, and rising silently Terence followed her, unseen. From the dark, he watched her arrange her things and lay out her blankets for bed. Just before she began to undress,

Terence slipped behind her and said softly, "Nurse Thessala?"

The elderly lady squawked and leaped several inches into the air. "Who? Squire Terence! How did you? I never heard —"

"I was just passing by, my lady," Terence began, "and thought I would ask you something I've been curious about."

"Oh! But you frightened me so! How could you — ?"

"What exactly did you give the regent this evening before bed?"

"Oh, that! Why, it's a tonic! It . . . it gives him . . . vigor and helps him to sleep!"

"Both at once?"

Thessala looked flustered for a moment, but as at the wedding ball, her pride in her own magical skills overcame her reluctance to speak. "Well, if you must know, that was the Elixer of Good Dreams that I told you about. The regent drinks it every night before bed, and while he sleeps he dreams that he is embraced by his adoring wife."

"But he isn't."

"Oh, no. But the regent believes it, and it keeps him happy, as you've seen." Thessala allowed herself a little titter. "He says that Fenice holds him *exactly* as his former wife used to. Isn't that sweet?"

"And that's what you call happiness?"

"Of course. Because, if you must know, Fenice doesn't really like him very much. If he knew the truth, he would be so miserable! It's best this way, for everyone."

"Best for Alis?" Terence demanded, incredulous. "Best that he doesn't know that his wife loves Cligés?"

Thessala nodded eagerly. "Exactly! It's perfect, don't you think? Everyone has what they want!"

"Or believes that they do," Terence said.

"It's the same thing," Thessala responded, smiling. "If you *think* you're happy, then you are!"

Terence shook his head slowly but didn't reply. Instead he faded silently into the shadows and began moving back toward his own blankets. After some fifty yards, he heard someone in deep conversation among the trees and recognized the voices of Cligés and Fenice. He glanced involuntarily toward the camp, where he could make out the shape of the regent's wagon in the flickering firelight. He supposed Alis was inside dreaming that Fenice was beside him. He returned to his own gear and found Dinadan already stretched out there.

"Where've you been?" Dinadan asked.

"Talking with that nurse," Terence said wearily. "I'll tell you about it later."

"All right," Dinadan replied. "But I thought I'd tell you the news."

"News?"

"Just after you slipped away, a horseman came down the path, riding hard away from Mainz."

"Yes?"

"He says that the emperor and duke are in all-out war now, that they've already begun attacking each other's serfs and towns. Maybe a thousand peasants killed so far."

Terence raised his eyes and looked back into the black shadows of the woods where Cligés and Fenice were huddled together, blissfully absorbed in their world of young love, and there was nothing to say and no words with which to say it.

10

QUESTING

By the time the caravan crossed back into lands held by the empire, the imperial court had lost its fascination with the peculiar nature of Alis and Fenice's marriage. When Alis began extolling the virtues of his loving bride — as he continued to do — the Greek courtiers no longer showed any discomfort, or interest. When Cligés and Fenice spoke endearingly to each other or gazed soulfully into each other's eyes or went off alone for more intimate expressions of love, those who witnessed the two lovers would, at most, roll their eyes and shake their heads.

Only Terence tried to resist this accepting attitude. "The thing is," he said to Dinadan and Acoriondes, "it's still wrong! It doesn't matter that everyone's taking it for granted now; Cligés is betraying his kinsman, and Fenice is betraying her wedding vows. And don't you think it's wrong for Alis to go on living a lie?"

Acoriondes shook his head and smiled affectionately at Terence. "My friend, you amaze me. In many ways you are wiser than anyone I have met, and yet you know so little about falsehood."

"Thank you, I think," Terence replied.

"Do you imagine that there is anyone who does not live a lie? Pretend to be what he is not? I have no doubt that you yourself live so."

"I can't think of anything that I pretend —"

"But that is my point," Acoriondes interrupted. "We are none of us aware of our own lies. Lies only appear false when they are new. Old and time-honored lies are simply the way things are. We grow accustomed to them, learn to honor and cherish them, and in the end fight with all our might to defend them."

"From what?"

"From the truth, of course."

Terence pondered this doubtfully. Did he really live with lies that he wasn't even aware of? In the silence, Dinadan yawned and said, "Come now, Terence. Surely this isn't new to you. Lies are the stones that we build kingdoms from. Look at old Karl and the Duke of Saxony — making up lies about honor and loyalty when all they really wanted was wealth and power. But in the end, they started believing their own lies and now are fighting a war to defend honor that they never had, destroying each other in grand gestures, because if they didn't they'd have to admit their own littleness."

Acoriondes nodded approvingly at Dinadan. "You surprise me, Sir Dinadan. I did not think you very wise when I first met you, but you see the world more clearly than I thought."

Dinadan shrugged. "I'm a poet," he said shortly. "Poets are allowed to speak the truth because no one takes them seriously."

Acoriondes's smile deepened. "There is something in what you say. Perhaps poets are actually prophets."

"Lord, don't let that idea get around," Dinadan said hastily. "Prophets get crucified."

After a pensive moment, Acoriondes commented, "There used to be one prophet who did not — in ancient Greece, and not very far out of our path. You know, before this German wedding business came up, I said I wanted to show you the wonders of Greece. Why should we not begin at Delphi?"

"What is Delphi?" Terence asked.

"It was an ancient oracle to the pagan god Apollo," Acoriondes explained. "There are still magnificent ruins there. It is on Mount Parnassus, which we will pass in a day or two. Shall we leave the rest of the group and visit it?"

"I've heard of Delphi," Dinadan said. "There was a priestess there, right?"

"The Pythia, yes."

"And she would inquire of Apollo at some sort of cave, which was supposed to be a gateway between worlds."

"Something of the sort was said," Acoriondes agreed. "But really, the ruins of the temple and the theater are what you should see."

Terence cared little for ruins, but the phrase *gateway between worlds* had not escaped him. "Let's go," he said.

It was already dusk when the three friends arrived at the deserted site of the Delphic oracle. For the past hour, Terence had felt an uncanny excitement growing in him. In England he had occasionally come upon gateways between worlds, places where the boundaries of the World of Men and the World of the Faeries overlapped, but never had he felt the breath of another world so powerfully. Just at sunset, they climbed a ledge and beheld the ruined temple of Apollo. Thick stone pillars supporting nothing pointed toward heaven like accusing fingers, black against the orange sky. Tumbledown stones overgrown with gray shrubs seemed to be everywhere. "Where is that cave?" Terence asked.

"The oracle itself?" Acoriondes asked. "No one knows for certain. It could have been any hole in the ground, really." His voice sounded weary. Terence realized that in his growing eagerness he had led his friends up the mountain at a punishing pace. Because they would be climbing, they had come on foot, leaving their horses in the care of Acoriondes's squire Bernard. Terence still felt full of energy himself, but the others had to be exhausted.

"Let's make camp and rest," he said at once. "We can explore the ruins tomorrow, in the light." They found a slab of flat stone on which to build a fire, then stretched out around it to stare into the flames and talk, if they wished to, or simply to be silent. Having that choice had been the nicest part of going off alone, Terence reflected. In a crowd, there was always pressure to make conversation, for fear of seeming rude, but with real friends, silence is also acceptable. Terence allowed himself to relax, feeling the light and warmth of the fire on his face and the cool emptiness of darkness behind him, and enjoying both at the same time. Dinadan took out his rebec, tuned it, then began playing a quiet air in the darkness.

"You are a strange man, Sir Dinadan," murmured Acoriondes sleepily. "You are a knight, yet you have more skill in music than any minstrel I have ever known."

Dinadan evidently felt that this observation required no answer and merely continued playing. Acoriondes lay back on his blankets, but Terence remained wakeful. The air of Delphi smelled of life and excitement and mystery, and Dinadan's quavering melody seemed to stir the space into dancing, unfamiliar patterns. Terence closed his eyes to sharpen his sense of hearing.

"What is that melody, Dinadan?" Terence asked. "I've never heard it before, have I?"

"I call it 'Song for Rhiannon,'" Dinadan replied softly. "I composed it many years ago, for an unhappy young bride."

"I've never heard its like," Terence said. "It's like a call to a deeper place."

Dinadan didn't reply, but continued playing for several more minutes. Involuntary shivers convulsed Terence's spine, and he allowed himself to relax and know the hair-prickling sensation of the presence of genius. The trees began to rustle and whistle breathily, though Terence felt no wind on his face and none disturbed the fire. Then Dinadan stopped playing and cocked his head to listen. For a long moment there was no sound but a faint snore from the prone figure of Acoriondes; then the wind began again with an eerie whistle that sounded oddly similar to the notes that Dinadan had just played. Dinadan smiled broadly.

"Is he asleep?" asked a quiet voice in the blackness.

"Sylvanus?" asked Dinadan.

"I told you we would make music together again," replied the quiet voice. A moment later a patch of darkness in the general shape of a person appeared against the blue-gray sky.

"Terence," Dinadan said. "Allow me to introduce you to an old friend, Sylvanus."

Terence didn't have to ask if this Sylvanus was from another world; he had already noted the faint suggestion of horns on the silhouetted head and the faint clicking of hooves on the stone slab. "I am honored," Terence said. "Is, er, Sylvanus your only name?"

Sylvanus chuckled. "Ah, now that's a knowing sort of question. I had a *feeling* about you as I came near. You know: the sense that here's someone who has traveled between worlds. As you have guessed, I do have many names. But who are you? Terence is a good Roman name, but I don't know you. What world are you from?"

Terence hesitated only a second. He normally wouldn't talk about his otherworldly connections before Dinadan, but if Dinadan was a friend of this creature, then he could trust him. "Avalon."

"Ganscotter's world," Sylvanus said.

"My father," Terence replied, nodding.

Sylvanus swept a low bow before Terence. "I am honored, sir. We of Elysium know and revere your

214

father's name." Then Sylvanus rose again to his full height and turned to Dinadan. "And why have you been calling me, my old friend?"

"I didn't know I *was*, actually," Dinadan replied. "I was just playing what felt right. Terence? Are you not really from this world? I mean, aren't you human?"

"Half," Terence assured him. "And I *was* born in this world. In Lancashire."

"But your father's a . . . what, a faery?"

"A lot of people have faery blood," Terence explained. "Gawain does, even Arthur. I just have more than most."

Sylvanus spoke again. "But if you didn't call me, my friend, who did? *Someone* was certainly doing so," Sylvanus said. "My lord Terence?"

Terence nodded slowly. "I suppose you could say I was calling," he admitted. "Not you, particularly, mind you. But I've been looking for answers from beyond this world."

"Why not ask your father?"

Terence frowned. "Avalon is silent," he said. "There's been no traffic between the worlds for many months — no word, nothing. That's what I'm looking for. I want to know why. Do you know . . . or is there someone in your world who might know what is going on in mine?"

Sylvanus considered this. "Perhaps," he admitted. "There is one who sees into more worlds than any of us. But that one never comes here anymore. I would have to take you to Elysium."

Terence stood at once. "If you would, friend Sylvanus, I would be deeply grateful."

Sylvanus smiled. "Very well. Dinadan? Do you come with us or stay here?"

"You must be joking," Dinadan said at once, rising to his feet.

"And what about our friend?" Terence asked, nodding at the still figure of Acoriondes.

"Don't worry. He'll sleep safely until your return."

A moment later they were gone, picking their way through the jumbled masonry. Sylvanus skipped lightly along a path that Terence couldn't even see in the gloom, but neither he nor Dinadan stumbled in the dark. "So, Sylvanus?" Dinadan asked as they walked. "If that's only one of your names, then what else are you called?"

"I been most often called Dionysos," the shadowy figure replied over his shoulder.

"Dionysos?" Dinadan exclaimed. "Isn't that the god of wine?"

"*God* is such a limiting word," Sylvanus complained. "People think they know what it means and then expect all sorts of nonsense from you."

"All the same, you're *that* Dionysos?"

"In past days, people certainly called me the god of

216

wine," Sylvanus admitted. "That's why I don't use that name anymore. When people hear 'Dionysos' they think only of drunken revels. Really, there's more to me than wine. In fact, when I first began visiting this world, in Thrace, people didn't call me that at all."

"Oh? What did those people call you?" asked Dinadan.

"The god of beer." Sylvanus stopped at what looked like a sheer wall. "Here we are. The cave of the oracle." Then, before Terence's astonished eyes, Sylvanus stepped into the rock.

"Terence?" Dinadan whispered.

"I didn't see it either," Terence replied. "Come on. And let's join hands."

Together they moved to the place where they had last seen Sylvanus. The wall before them could not have seemed more solid, but taking a deep breath, Terence stepped into it, pulling Dinadan along with him. No rock touched them, and in a moment they stood in pitch darkness.

"So that's why no one knows where the oracle was," Dinadan commented. "It doesn't actually look much like a cave."

"Sheer provincialism," said Sylvanus's voice from a few feet away. "People always expect other worlds to have the same rules as their own. Why should a cave into my world look like a cave in yours? Come along."

They walked in darkness for several minutes, until a faint red glow appeared before them, gradually lighting their path. Before long, they could see the walls on either side — not jagged rock but walls of polished white stone — and a few minutes later the smooth rock path became soft as their feet began crunching across gravel. A wide ribbon of pitch blackness crossed their path. "A river?" Terence asked.

"The River Styx," Sylvanus replied. "Wait a moment: the boatman's coming."

A movement of darkness flickered before Terence's eyes, and the shape of a long boat with a standing ferryman appeared, as if rising from beneath the surface of the river itself. A voice growled something, and Sylvanus said, "English, please."

"Ainglish?" grunted the new voice. "Ye've brought Ainglish? Is summat wrong wi' yer head?"

"Just take us across," Sylvanus replied quietly.

"Gaffers ain't dead yet!"

"Don't be an idiot. Just take us across. And don't try that silly old lie about how the weight of the living will sink your boat."

"Serve ye roight if it did," the boatman muttered, but he stepped back and made room for the three travelers. They crossed the river in silence but for the boatman's subdued muttering about how he'd never seen an Englishman before and didn't care to see any more if these two were what they were like. Sylvanus led Terence and Dinadan onto the shore, and boatman and boat disappeared silently behind them.

"Pleasant chap," Dinadan remarked.

"I've often thought that it must be exhausting to keep up such an attitude," Sylvanus said, "but Charon never disappoints me."

"If he's never seen an Englishman before," Terence asked, "how is it that he speaks English?"

"Would you call that English?" Dinadan murmured.

Sylvanus smiled. "Many of the barriers that divide humans from each other are unimportant here, my lord Terence." Then he turned to Dinadan. "Charon's English *was* rather odd, wasn't it?"

"What would you say, Terence? Yorkshire?"

"Maybe," Terence agreed. "Northern, anyway."

Sylvanus chuckled. "Hardly surprising," he said. "You should hear his Greek. Fellow has a dreadful Macedonian accent."

"Why was he surprised that we weren't dead?" Terence asked.

"Most who make this journey are," Sylvanus explained. "You'll meet some former residents of your world before long, I imagine. But don't be disturbed by his ill temper; Charon's often given rides to the living, coming *and* going. Step this way. We'll need to hunt around a bit to find the one we're looking for."

They went on together toward the growing red light, and after several minutes Terence heard the sharp tapping of goat hooves approaching. "Pan?" called Sylvanus. "Is that you?"

"Here, master," piped a shrill voice. "What in heaven's name have you there?"

"Lord Terence of Avalon and Sir Dinadan of England," Sylvanus replied. "We're looking for the Old One. Have you seen him?"

"She hasn't been around recently," the voice replied. "In one of his moods, I would guess. Are you really from Avalon?"

Assuming that this was addressed to him, Terence replied, "I am."

"Delightful!" the voice cried, and a skipping goat-legged figure no more than three feet high appeared and began dancing around Terence. "I've an old friend there, I have! Perhaps you know him? Pook?"

Terence nodded. His friend Robin often went by the name Puck. "I do. I'm afraid I haven't seen him in a long time, though. Shall I give him your greetings when I do, Master Pan?"

"Give him my greetings?" the little figure asked. "Whatever for?"

Terence hesitated as he realized that he had no idea what purpose a secondhand greeting might serve. "I don't know. It's just something that people do."

"A good enough reason not to do it, I would think," Pan chirped. He turned back to Sylvanus. "You might look in the lower region. Dismal place, but if the Old One's in a funk, she might go there."

Sylvanus nodded and turned off the path to his right. "This way, friends," he said. "And if we go quickly, we might slip by the Thirsty."

Terence exchanged a glance with Dinadan, but neither asked for an explanation of this ominous-sounding designation. They trotted behind Sylvanus down a long slope. "I say, Sylvanus," called Dinadan.

"Yes?"

"This 'Old One' we're looking for — is it a man or a woman?"

"Very likely," Sylvanus replied. "Watch your step, there."

Terence and Dinadan had to veer sharply to the right to keep from stepping into a stream that flowed sluggishly downhill beside them, carrying thick clumps over the rocks to plop loudly into viscous pools. "Eugh!" muttered Dinadan at Terence's side. "No wonder someone's thirsty here, if the water's like that."

"Oh, that's not water," Sylvanus called over his shoulder. "That's blood. It must be a peaceful day in your world. When you're having a war, this stream's a torrent. Hurry, now . . . Oh, blast! Never mind."

A moment later, the three travelers were surrounded by flitting, gibbering phantoms stretching their arms toward Terence and Dinadan and kneeling at their feet. The shadowy, insubstantial figures opened their mouths like baby birds, gaping and closing, gaping and closing, all the while pleading in Greek. Terence halted, unwilling to push the figures out of his way, and sensed Dinadan doing the same. "These are the Thirsty, I suppose?" Dinadan asked Sylvanus.

As soon as Dinadan spoke, the figures shifted to English. "Please, sirs, a drink! I beg you! Give me once again a taste of what you know always! A drink! Give me life, though only for a moment! A drink, a drink!" But the figures seemed to have strength enough only for a few words, and after speaking would collapse to the ground, only to be climbed over by others gasping out the same plea.

"I have no water," Terence said kindly.

"They don't want water," Sylvanus said. Terence looked at their guide, then glanced incredulously at the stream of blood that ran beside them. "That's right," Sylvanus said. "These are some of those who have come here after death."

"And they want blood?" Dinadan asked. "Is this what death is like?"

"Only for them," Sylvanus explained. "These shades, when they were alive in your world, existed by sucking life from others. Here are the callous rich, the wheedling poor, domineering husbands and wives, hypochondriacs, beggars, princes, bishops. All sorts are here, existing exactly as they did in life, but without their pretenses. Here they live forever in their natural state."

"Live forever?" Dinadan repeated.

"Oh, yes, my friend. The only thing that dies in Elysium is a lie."

Terence felt his gorge rising, but he fought down his nausea. "And they want blood to drink? Why don't they just drink from the stream?"

Sylvanus shook his head. "They are only able to drink what someone else gives them. Justice is often cruel."

"And if someone gives them a drink of blood?"

Sylvanus shrugged. "For a few fleeting moments, they feel a surge of strength."

Terence turned toward the throng and picked out a tall young shade who stood near the front. Alone of all the jostling shadows, he didn't gape his mouth or cry pitifully for blood. There was an empty cruelty in his eyes that Terence couldn't look at without feeling sick, but he seemed stronger than the rest. "You!" Terence said. "If I give you a drink, will you answer my questions?" The shade hesitated proudly, then nodded once. "Vow it!" Terence demanded. The phantom nodded again, and Terence knelt beside the clotted stream and dipped his hands into the gore. All the shades around him wailed and threw themselves forward, but Terence ignored them and took his cupped hands to the tall shade, who tilted his head and let Terence pour a mouthful of blood past his lips. At once the young man grew more solid and took on color. Closing his eyes, he drew a deep breath.

"Your name?" Terence snapped.

"I am Alexander." Terence blinked and stared more closely, but this was not the Alexander he knew, the emperor who had loved Sarah.

"Ask quickly, Lord Terence," whispered Sylvanus.

"We are looking for the Old One. Is he . . . er, or she, below?"

"Yes," the shade said. His face was already growing gray.

"Where?"

"By the rock of . . . of . . ." Then Alexander crumpled and almost disappeared from sight.

"Come," said Sylvanus, plucking at Terence's sleeve. "You won't get anything else from him."

They set out down the path, and the crowd of shadows turned away from them to pounce instead on the faint shape of Alexander, as if they meant to tear the young man apart and suck every last drop of blood from his shadow.

Dinadan glanced over his shoulder at the pawing and scratching mob. "Was that . . . Alexander the Great?" he asked.

"Did he look great to you?" Sylvanus replied.

"Did his information help at all?" Terence asked.

"Perhaps," Sylvanus said. "He never finished telling us which rock he meant, but there are only two or three rocks in the lower region that are notable enough to use as a landmark. I'm going to bet it's the rock of Sisyphus. Now I think of it, I recall seeing the Old One there before."

It was never easy to judge time when visiting other worlds, Terence knew, so he didn't ask how much longer it would be. Instead, he concentrated on placing his feet firmly in the path behind his guide to Lower Elysium. At last — though it could, of course, have been only a moment — the path opened out to a wide valley, dimly lit by a reddish orb that hung in the air above it, like a dying underground moon. There was a vast lake at the far end of the valley, and to their left there rose a long, conical hill up which a man was pushing a jagged boulder. "That's Sisyphus," Sylvanus said. "And there she is, the Old One. Just at the foot of the hill."

Together they approached. The Old One sat quietly on what appeared to be the bones of a huge creature. He was bald and had a tangled gray beard. "There, Dinadan," Terence said. "The Old One's a man."

"You're sure?" Dinadan said. "Look at her chest."

Terence looked more closely and saw that the Old One's loosely gaping robe clearly revealed the withered

225

breasts of an old woman. Sylvanus chuckled. "We don't even wonder anymore. We just take him as she is. But whatever else you can say about her, she knows more than any of us. The trick is getting him to say what he knows." Sylvanus stopped about a stone's throw from the Old One, and said, "You go on, Lord Terence. She's more likely to speak to a lone questioner."

Leaving the others behind, Terence walked up to the Old One. He sensed that he was being closely observed, but as he approached he realized that the Old One's eyes were blank and covered with a thick white film. "And what," rasped the Old One, "brings the Duke of Avalon to Elysium?"

Despite all that Sylvanus had said, Terence was mildly surprised at being recognized, especially by his rank. He often went months at a time without thinking of his official title himself. "I'm looking for you, sir. Or madam."

"You may call me sir," the Old One said. "I feel more a man today. Or you could use my name. I am Tieresias. Why do you seek me?"

"If you know that I am from Avalon, you know that I have frequent communication with my father, Ganscotter, both in person and through messengers."

Tieresias yawned. "Is that so?"

"But all that communication has stopped. I have heard nothing at all from Avalon for most of a year."

"So?"

"I am anxious. Just before Avalon grew silent, my father told me that there had been a deep plot laid against my king — Arthur of Britain. I am afraid that the one who has laid that plot is also preventing me from speaking to those beyond the World of Men."

Tieresias shrugged. "It could be. There are those who have such power."

"Is it so? And who is it?"

"Why do you care?"

"Arthur is my king and friend. If there are plots against him, I want to protect him."

"Why?" Terence blinked at this, and Tieresias went on. "Do you suppose that you can prevent your Arthur from dying, or his kingdom from collapsing? You cannot."

"I can keep it from happening now."

"Now, next year, ten years from now . . . *when* means nothing. Look about you. In this place, do you think that ten years matters? Arthur will die. Your master Gawain will die. You will die. Arthur's kingdom will fall and be replaced by another, like every kingdom and empire before Arthur's and after. In the end, the time it happens matters not at all. You waste my energy with childish questions. Go away."

Terence stood uncertainly before Tieresias, feeling the weight of the Old One's own jaded weariness settling on his own shoulders. Behind Tieresias, on the conical hill, the man who had been pushing the large rock arrived at the summit. The rock quivered on the top for a moment, then rolled down the other side. The man took a breath and followed it down the slope. At the bottom, he set his shoulder to the stone and began pushing it back toward the hill. Terence turned to Tieresias.

"Sir, perhaps you are right. But I still wish to serve Arthur. If I can help him against his enemies, I will do what I can."

The Old One shrugged. "You may do what you like, but why should I pretend to care about what does not matter?"

"You don't have to care, sir, but you have knowledge that might help me."

"And why should I care if I help you? Go away, I said." Tieresias bowed his head and rested it on his staff, to all appearances sound asleep. Terence stared at him helplessly, unable to think of any more arguments. It occurred to him that perhaps the Old One was right. Maybe trying to change the course of history was pointless.

Then a new noise intruded on his despondent reflections: a faint but cheerful whistle. Terence blinked and looked around, seeing nothing. He looked behind Tieresias and realized that the whistle was coming from the man pushing the rock up the hill. The cheerful little tune broke off abruptly as Sisyphus braced his shoulders against the boulder and muscled it over a bump in the hill's surface, but then it resumed. Terence looked back at Tieresias, then again at Sisyphus, and leaving the Old One he walked up the hill toward man and rock.

Still whistling, Sisyphus gave Terence a welcoming nod, but he didn't speak. Instead he bent his knees, braced his shoulders against the stone, and began pushing it up. The whistling broke off for a second, but the rock didn't move. Without thinking, Terence stepped up beside Sisyphus and began pushing with him. The stone seemed almost to push back, but after a moment the gravel beneath it slipped, and it lurched a few more inches upward. Terence found himself breathing heavily from the exertion and heard Sisyphus panting beside him, but neither spoke. Sisyphus braced himself again; Terence joined him. Again they forced the rock uphill. And then again. Between shoves, Sisyphus would resume his whistle. Terence suddenly grinned and, once he was sure of the tune, began to whistle with him. Side by side they grunted and whistled and heaved until at last they had the boulder again at the top, where it balanced precariously for a second, then rolled down the other side.

Terence watched it until it had stopped, then said, "And now you go get it again?"

"Yes," Sisyphus replied pleasantly, starting down the slope.

Terence fell into step beside him. "Why?" he asked. Sisyphus only shrugged. "To push a rock up a hill only to have to do it again is . . . it's —"

"Absurd?" supplied Sisyphus.

"Yes, absurd."

"And your life is not?"

Terence didn't reply. They walked together in silence for several seconds. They came to the rock, and Sisyphus braced his shoulders against it. "But if you know it's absurd," Terence said, "why do you do it?"

Sisyphus grinned. "The task is absurd. So are they all. But I am not my task. I am more. I am Sisyphus." With that he grunted and began rolling his burden back toward the hill.

Slowly Terence nodded, then with chin lifted he walked back around the hill to where Tieresias still sat. "Sir," Terence said. "I ask again. Who is preventing other worlds from entering Britain now, and what is the plot that has been laid against my king?"

The Old One sighed. "And I reply again. Who cares?"

"I care."

"Why?"

"Because to serve my friends is who I am. Not to do so is to deny myself. You called me the Duke of

Avalon: do not do so again. I am more than that. I am Terence."

Tieresias was still for a long moment, then nodded. "I am glad to meet you. The plot against Arthur was laid by his half-sister Morgause, who sometimes calls herself the Enchantress." Terence nodded. He had been nearly certain of that already. Tieresias went on. "It is she who has cast a spell over your land, shutting the gates to otherworldly voices. The spell cannot last long, but it will last long enough for her plot to succeed."

"And what is her plot?"

"Did you not hear me? It will succeed. The end of Arthur's kingdom is in sight."

"Did you not hear me? I don't stand with Arthur because I believe he can win. I stand with him because I will not do otherwise. What is the plot?"

"She has sent her son to Camelot, to infiltrate the Round Table and to drag the king down by guile and dissension."

"Her son?" Terence said, horror slowly filling his breast.

"Yes. Her son: conceived by guile and enchantment many years ago, and raised in hatred too pure for any mortal to withstand. That son is now hardly human at all — a man filled with such a deep well of hatred that he is capable of poisoning a great emperor merely from spite."

"Poisoning an emperor?" Terence repeated. "Alexander?"

"Yes, merely because Alexander was wise and just and averted a war that the boy might have enjoyed watching."

"What is this son's name?" Terence asked grimly.

"You already know, Terence."

Terence nodded. "Mordred," he said.

11

THE COURTLY LOVE
OF CLIGÉS AND FENICE

Sylvanus left Terence and Dinadan at the cave of the oracle. One moment he was there, chuckling and bidding them an excellent morning, and the next he was gone, and the wall of the cave was again sheer and impenetrable rock. Dinadan felt the surface, then turned and looked around them. It was early morning, and birds whistled and chirped among the tiny buds that were beginning to show on the trees.

"Terence? You've traveled between worlds before," Dinadan began. "Does it always feel so discouraging to return?"

"Discouraging?"

"Coming back to this world — it's so flat and colorless."

Terence frowned. "Dinadan, we've just come out of a cave into the open air. How can you say that it's colorless?" In fact, Terence had just been noting that Delphi had much more color than when they had left. Surely the trees had not been budding then?

"I didn't mean that kind of color," Dinadan said. "But does it always feel strange to return?"

Terence nodded, deciding not to explain in any more detail until his suspicions were confirmed. "Come on. Let's find old Acoriondes."

As Sylvanus had promised, Acoriondes was still asleep, in exactly the same position in which they had left him. The only difference was in his beard. Usually closely trimmed, Acoriondes's beard hung in wild, grizzled tangles, almost to the ground. *A month, maybe?* Terence thought, considering the whiskers. *Six weeks?*

"Terence? Look at the fire," Dinadan said. Where they had made their fire the night before, there were only one or two slightly blackened sticks to show it had ever been there. In its place grew several inches of new spring grass, poking out of cracks in the ancient stone. Dinadan looked intently at him. "Terence?"

"Sometimes," Terence explained, "when you visit another world, you come back to find that time has been moving on without you in this one."

"How *much* time?"

"Once Gawain and I were gone for a few months and came back seven years later. That was before you got to court. But I don't think it's so bad this time. It's obviously spring, but it's the same year. We should build a fire and make some breakfast. When Acoriondes wakes up, he'll be hungry."

Dinadan built the fire and fetched water while Terence scouted the area for food. The dried food that had been in their packs was long gone, foraged by small animals and birds, so he took his bow and arrows and was able to kill a wild goat that he found among the rocks. On his way back to camp, passing by the now closed door of the oracle, he found a thick vine covered with ripe grapes and gathered an armload to bring along. By the time Acoriondes began to stir and stretch, the meat was nearly cooked. "I must have been very tired," the counselor said. "I slept soundly."

Neither Terence nor Dinadan replied. Together they breakfasted on roast meat and grapes. Acoriondes examined the grapes without comment, but ate ravenously. At last he said, "What happened to our bread?"

"I think some animals got into it," Terence said. "It's all gone."

"Hmm."

Dinadan glanced at Terence and with one raised eyebrow indicated clearly that he thought Terence ought to say something.

"And fresh grapes, too," Acoriondes mused. "Odd, in late winter, don't you think?"

Terence nodded.

"Except that it doesn't seem to be winter any longer, does it?"

Terence took a breath. "You yourself said that this place had been considered uncanny. It does appear that, by some mysterious power, what felt like one night to us has lasted for several weeks."

Acoriondes pondered this. "And the grapes?"

"That I can't explain," Terence said. "If I were one of the ancient Greeks, who believed in the pagan gods, I would say that we had been given a gift by the god of wine."

"*God* is such a limiting word," Dinadan murmured.

For another few minutes, they ate in silence. At last Acoriondes said, "It would seem that you are correct and that several weeks are past. Forgive me, but would you be angry if I cut short our traveling? I find that I am anxious about the regent and the court in Athens."

"No, indeed," Terence replied promptly. "I feel the same way about Arthur and England. I will return with you to Athens to get my horse, but will leave at once for my own land." He glanced at Dinadan inquiringly.

"Not unless you need me," Dinadan said. "I still want to learn Greek, and there are new lands and languages to visit from here."

Terence nodded. He would have been glad of the

company on the return, but in other ways he was relieved. Terence had not told Dinadan what he had learned from Tieresias and wasn't sure he would be able to, at least in its full significance. Like Arthur, Gawain, Lancelot, and Kai, Terence had promised not to reveal that Mordred was Arthur's son. Without that knowledge, the information that Mordred was also the son of Arthur's greatest enemy carried less meaning. As much as Terence had learned to appreciate Dinadan on this journey, he would be glad to finish his travels alone.

By inquiring obliquely in villages along the way, the three friends determined that just over a month had passed since they had separated from the imperial party. Twice, in small taverns, Acoriondes overheard snatches of gloomy conversation about the "upset" at the court, and once he heard someone talking about the Caliph's army. Acoriondes explained that the Caliph was the ruler of the Seljuk Empire, a powerful realm east of Constantinople, but he forebore to ask for further information from the townspeople. "By the time the story gets to the taverns," he explained, "it has probably been distorted beyond recognition. All we can be certain of is that matters are unsettled, both at court and on the frontiers."

They were able to obtain more direct information

soon. On the outskirts of Athens, they came upon a wide field where a courtier was hunting with a falcon. When they drew near, the falconer looked up, then cried joyously, *"Kyrie!"* and ran with outstretched arms toward them. It was Bernard. For nearly an hour, Acoriondes and his squire sat beside the road and spoke quickly and urgently in their own language. Watching them, Terence could tell only that startling events had taken place. Acoriondes's sharp questions often bore a note of alarm, occasionally incredulity. Dinadan, too, blinked with surprise several times, and Terence guessed that he was understanding much of Bernard's speech.

At last Bernard finished his recital and answered all his master's questions. Acoriondes stood, "Come! We must go."

"You want to tell me what's going on?" Terence asked. "Is it Cligés and Fenice still?"

"Cligés and Fenice are dead," Acoriondes said.

Now it was Terence's turn to blink with surprise. "But how?"

"Fenice grew ill shortly after arriving in Athens. Nothing could help her."

"Not even her nurse? Thessala?" Terence asked.

"Not even she. Bernard says that a famous doctor of Salerno happened to arrive shortly after she took ill, but he, too, failed to cure her."

Dinadan cleared his throat. "That was one of the

bits I had trouble with, actually," he said. "I must be getting similar words confused, but it sounded to me as if Bernard said that Cligés threw the doctor into the sea."

"You understood that?" Acoriondes demanded.

"If that's really what he said," Dinadan replied. "But why — ?"

"Bernard isn't certain himself. It seems that the doctor told Alis that he knew exactly what was wrong with Fenice and could cure her, if he would only be allowed to treat her alone. So Alis banished everyone from the room, and sure enough the doctor had her back on her feet within an hour. But then, it appears, Fenice told Thessala that the doctor had tortured her cruelly while they were alone. When Cligés heard that, he went to the doctor in a rage and threw him from a window, at a spot where the palace goes up to the edge of a cliff. They never found the doctor's remains. The next day, Fenice took ill again."

"Did she, now?" Terence said softly.

"Two days later, she died. Bernard says that Alis is inconsolable, has not eaten or drunk enough to keep a dog alive, and goes every day to weep for an hour outside her tomb. He cares neither for himself nor for the empire, but seems only to long for death."

Bernard pointed away to the north, where a white marble tower jutted above the level of the low trees, and said something. Acoriondes examined the marble

239

turret for a moment, then interpreted. "Bernard says that is the top of Fenice's tomb. It was built as a summer home for a wealthy merchant, but Fenice had seen and admired it. On her deathbed, she asked that Alis buy that home, leave her body there, and wall it up without doors or windows for eternity."

"And he did?" Dinadan asked.

"At great expense to the imperial treasury," Acoriondes added.

"But wait," Terence said suddenly. "You said that Cligés was dead, too."

"Yes, would you explain that?" added Dinadan. "That's another part I didn't get."

"I didn't at first, either," Acoriondes said. He drew a deep breath, then said, "Once Fenice was gone, Cligés made no effort to hide his love for her."

"I hadn't noticed any particular effort before," Dinadan said.

"Nor I, but it grew worse. He wailed and moaned and tore his clothes and outmourned his uncle. Then, on the day of the funeral, when Fenice's coffin was carried to the tomb and walled up inside, Cligés was nowhere to be found."

"Eugh!" Dinadan said. "You mean he was hiding inside the tomb?"

"Not in the tomb," Acoriondes said. "Thessala and Alis both insisted that every corner of the old house and garden be searched before the gates in the walls were sealed. No one was there."

"Then where — ?" Terence began.

"Two weeks later, a note was found in Cligés's room, hidden so that it would not be discovered right away," Acoriondes went on. "In the note, Cligés told what he was going to do. Apparently the night before the funeral he sealed himself inside the coffin with Fenice."

There was a long silence. "Now, that's ugly," Dinadan said at last.

Acoriondes wore his expressionless face. "He said he wanted to spend eternity with his love," he finished tonelessly.

"And what if the blithering ass changed his mind after he was sealed in?" Dinadan wondered aloud.

"I believe it is best not to think about it," Acoriondes said.

"Oh, right. I'll just think happy thoughts instead," Dinadan replied. "Do you think they wore matching outfits? That would be adorable!"

"Shut up, Dinadan," said Terence. "Bernard?"

"Yes, Squire Terence?" Bernard replied, in halting English.

"Do you think that you could show me Fenice's tomb?"

Bernard glanced at Acoriondes, who translated for him. "But yes, Squire Terence. When?"

"At once," Terence replied. He looked up at Aco-riondes and said, "You go to the regent. He needs you. But if you could spare Bernard for a while, I would like to see this tomb."

"How will you understand each other?"

"Bernard has some English. Dinadan has some Greek. We'll join you shortly."

"As you wish," Acoriondes replied. He struck off down the road toward the palace, while Bernard led the others through the thinly forested area to the north. Perhaps because of the language differences, they made the trip in complete silence but for the sound of Bernard's and Dinadan's footsteps. Less than half an hour later, they stood outside Fenice's tomb.

It was a pleasant, rather ornate country villa built on a hill so as to catch the sea breezes, away from the dirt and heat of the city in summer. High stone walls rose from the forest floor, enclosing and concealing a wide area. At one end of the hidden area, a majestic marble tower jutted up, and on the other side a few trees showed above the wall. Terence pointed at the trees and said to Bernard, "Is there a garden on that side?"

Bernard hesitated, then nodded. "Yes, yes. A garden and a . . . *pege.*"

"A spring," Dinadan translated. "Shame to close up fresh water inside a tomb."

Bernard took a quick breath, and his eyes lit up as a

covey of quail, or some similar bird, rose with a loud drumming of wings from within the garden. Bernard's right hand stole toward his left arm, on which he still carried his hooded falcon. Terence caught his hand. "Another time," Terence said. "We are not here for hunting."

"Why *are* we here?" asked Dinadan.

"I was just curious," Terence said vaguely. "Let's walk around the walls."

It took them several minutes to complete the circuit—the enclosure was larger than it looked. They found the two former gates in the wall, now securely sealed with cut stone and mortar. They also found, by one of the closed gates, a wilting bouquet of flowers. Dinadan asked Bernard a question in hesitant Greek, listened to the reply, then said to Terence, "Alis. Bernard says he brings fresh flowers every day."

Terence nodded.

"Curious thing," Dinadan added. "Bernard says that the old nurse, Thessala, comes up every day as well."

"Why is that strange?" Terence asked. "Fenice had been her charge since she was born."

"Only one bunch of flowers," Dinadan pointed out.

Terence nodded again, and looking into Dinadan's eyes saw a reflection of his own suspicions. He glanced at Bernard and said, "Let's go now."

Terence and Dinadan spoke only of incidentals on the road to Athens, neither being sure how much English Bernard understood, but even after they arrived at the imperial palace they had no chance to talk privately. Acoriondes met them at the doorway and took them aside at once. His face was lined with deep anxiety.

"Alis is ill?" Terence asked.

"Alis is an idiot," Acoriondes replied shortly. "He has no thought for anything but his own grief. He says he will never leave Athens, never leave Fenice's tomb, never return to Constantinople."

Dinadan pursed his lips. "I suppose an emperor who never visits his capital isn't ideal."

"Especially when the Caliph is preparing for war in the east," Acoriondes said bitterly. "It seems that messengers from the eastern borders have been sending alarming messages for weeks now. Spies tell us of new military exercises, new weapons, and now even a new army brought in from Africa." The courtier hesitated, then said, "At least, we fear it is an army. A large caravan has arrived, anyway. The spies were not certain that all were soldiers, but the caravan was led by the most famous of all the Moorish warriors, a fierce knight named Palomides."

Dinadan was silent, but Terence said, "I've heard that name."

"Everyone has heard of him. He fought against your

own knights in Jerusalem. We fear that he has been brought in to lead a sneak attack, breaking the treaty between our empires."

"Oh, I wouldn't worry about that," Dinadan said calmly.

Acoriondes gave Dinadan an irritated look. "How can you say —?"

"I know Palomides. We rode together in England a while back."

Both Acoriondes and Terence stared at him. Terence said, "In England? But —"

"He never made it to Camelot."

"Why should we not fear Palomides?" Acoriondes demanded.

"If you go up against him in battle, you should jolly well fear him all you can. But if you're worried about sneak attacks and broken promises, you're wasting your time. Think of the most honorable man you've ever known. Now color his skin darker. That's Palomides."

Acoriondes looked hard at Dinadan for a moment, then relaxed visibly. "I have learned to trust your judgment, my friend. But we still must send a delegation to the Caliph to reaffirm the treaty, making sure that all is well. Alis can't be bothered, though. He has no thought for anything but picking flowers to take to that irritating girl's tomb."

"So send a delegation without Alis's permission," Dinadan said. Then he smiled. "I'd be glad of the company."

"Only the emperor can send a diplomatic mission. I cannot presume to —" Acoriondes began. Then he broke off and returned Dinadan's smile. "Ah, I see. You wish to visit your friend Palomides."

"Of course," Dinadan said. "And if you choose to send some trustworthy men with me — to show me the way, you understand — why, that would be most kind of you."

Acoriondes nodded. "And if, while they were at the Caliph's court, they took our greetings and some presents, that would be only good manners. How soon could you leave?"

"As soon as possible," Dinadan said. "I've missed my friend."

"I know just the men to send with you," Acoriondes said. "Good men. They don't speak English, I'm afraid, but they speak the language of Araby." Dinadan nodded. His smile had not faded. Acoriondes turned toward Terence. "And you will be leaving tomorrow as well, will you not?"

"Soon, anyway," Terence agreed. "But before I leave, I'd like to speak with Fenice's old nurse, Thessala."

"I wondered if that's what you were thinking," Dinadan said. "It seems mad, doesn't it?"

"It's no less likely for all that," Terence said. "Remember, this is Cligés and Fenice."

"What are you talking about?" demanded Acoriondes.

"I don't think they're dead," Terence said bluntly. "I think they faked Fenice's death — doubtless with the same sort of potion that they used back in Mainz to fake Cligés's illness — and now are living together behind the walls of her tomb."

"But how would they survive?"

"There must be a secret entrance," Terence said.

"Not for them to go out," Dinadan supplied. "For Thessala to go in — bringing food and whatever else they need. Bernard says she visits them every day."

"You have proof of this?"

"No," Terence replied. "But there was certainly something moving in the garden behind the walls, something that flushed out a flock of birds."

"A squirrel, another bird; it could have been anything," Acoriondes said.

"Yes."

Acoriondes frowned in silence. "But it does explain it all," Acoriondes admitted grudgingly. "How Cligés could seal himself into the coffin with Fenice, for instance: he knew she was alive. The nurse could open the coffin later. This means that the heir to the throne is still alive." His expression lightened somewhat.

Terence knew what he was thinking: Cligés may not

247

have been much of a prize as an emperor, but anything must have seemed better to Acoriondes than the doddering, lovesick Alis. He hated to crush this faint hope, but he had to. "My theory also explains why Cligés threw the doctor over the cliff."

The three friends were silent for a long moment.

"I hadn't thought of that," Dinadan said. "The doctor realized Fenice wasn't really dying, and he had to be silenced." He shook his head slowly. "You know, I even know where they got this sickly idea — from the story of Tristram and Iseult. They ran away from Iseult's husband, too, and went off to live in what they called the Love Grotto."

"I remember the tale," Acoriondes said grimly. "A minstrel sang it in Champagne when we were on our way to England. I remember thinking that such an idea was too stupid to be believed."

"And so it is," Dinadan said. "But like most of the stupidest ideas, it actually happened. Tristram and Iseult also attempted murder to hide their secret."

"Murder," Acoriondes repeated wearily. "So what do you suggest, Terence?"

"Good or bad," Terence said, "it is better to know the truth. In the morning, let's go look for ourselves."

Terence and Acoriondes weren't able to slip away from Athens until late morning, though. They waited to see off the delegation to the Caliph. The austere diplomats that Acoriondes had chosen for the journey looked somber, clearly conscious of the gravity of their mission, but Dinadan was in a rollicking good humor and eager to be on his way. Alis did not appear; his personal manservant said that he had spent a sleepless night and had only fallen asleep at dawn.

Shortly before noon, as they neared Fenice's tomb — or Cligés and Fenice's hideaway, if Terence's suspicions were correct — the stillness of the forest was shattered by a scream of terror, followed by an angry shout and a cry of anguish. Terence and Acoriondes spurred their horses forward, and outside the tomb's garden wall they came upon Cligés himself, clad only in a thin shift but holding a sword high above his head, about to bring it down on a prone form at his feet.

"Cligés!" rapped Acoriondes furiously, urging his horse to greater speed. Cligés looked up, and in that moment of hesitation Acoriondes's mount hit him with a shoulder and sent him sprawling in the underbrush. Terence threw himself from his own horse and raced to the person on the ground. It was Bernard, and he was horribly wounded. There were deep cuts on both his forearms, as if he had been warding off attack, but the worst wound was in his left leg, just below the knee. Terence had been in enough battles to know there would be no saving that leg. The bone was broken, and the skin nearly cut through. Bernard was screaming in agony and trying to reach down to his bloody leg. Terence had no time for gentle methods; drawing his dagger he first reversed it and with a well-placed blow with the hilt knocked Bernard senseless. Then he whipped his own belt from his waist and tied it roughly but tightly around Bernard's leg, slowing the bleeding. Gritting his teeth, Terence took up his dagger again and cut away the rest of the loose and dangling leg. Then he rose to his feet, his hands and legs dripping with Bernard's blood, and his eyes full of fury.

"Tell me why I should not kill you right now!" he said softly to Cligés, who was just then scrambling dazedly to his feet. Perhaps something in the very quietness of Terence's tone sank into Cligés's conciousness as shouting would not have. He took an involuntary step backwards.

"You have but a knife!" Cligés stammered. "I have a sword."

"It's more than Bernard had," Terence said. "Why? Why did you attack an unarmed squire? What had he done to you?"

"He . . . he climbed the wall, calling for his falcon. And he saw me and . . . he saw me in the garden."

"He saw you and Fenice," Terence said. "And so he had to be silenced."

"He would have ruined everything!"

Terence took a step forward, and Acoriondes intervened. "Will Bernard live?" he demanded.

"Maybe, I don't know," Terence said. "Longer than this vermin, anyway." Terence was vaguely aware of tears running down his face, and Cligés seemed clouded in a mist of red. Terence didn't remember ever feeling such rage.

"Why did he have to go hunting here?" Cligés moaned. "He could have taken his birds anywhere!"

"And what will you do now?" Acoriondes snapped at Cligés. "Will you kill us as well?"

"I am sorry, Acoriondes, but yes, I must!" Cligés said wildly.

"Try, then!" Terence said softly. Acoriondes drew his own short sword.

Cligés stepped forward resolutely but hesitated as a wail came from the woods, and then Fenice appeared, also barely clothed. Even in his fury, Terence was able to register that the secret entrance to the tomb must be a tunnel that came out among the trees. Fenice ran in front of Cligés and screamed, "No! You must not kill him! I will without him die!"

"You're already dead," Terence said.

"I love him!" Fenice screamed. "I love him! From the moment I see him, I love him! I have never another and will never another love!"

Time seemed to stop as Cligés and Fenice stared

defiantly at Acoriondes and Terence. Terence saw no way out of the impasse and was acutely aware that Bernard's chance to live was bleeding away behind him. Something had to break the frozen moment.

And then something did. Bushes rustled at Terence's left, and the portly figure of Alis, regent of Constantinople, emerged from the forest. He stopped abruptly, staring at Fenice, then dropped the posy of flowers he had been holding and walked slowly toward her.

"Phoenixa?" he whispered. No one would ever know how much Alis figured out during that brief walk, but he at least understood that Fenice had played him for a fool from the beginning. Alis's face grew still and empty, then hard, and as he stepped up beside his wife, he reached out and took her throat in his hands.

"No!" cried Cligés. Acoriondes and Terence leaped forward to pull Alis away, but Cligés was quicker. He thrust his sword into Alis's breast.

Acoriondes brought the hilt of his weapon down on Cligés's head, dropping him like a stone, while Terence struggled to pry Alis's death grip from Fenice's neck. At last, he succeeded, and stepped back from the three prostrate forms.

Neither Terence nor Acoriondes spoke for a long time. At last Acoriondes said, "Sophocles. It is like the final scene in a play by Sophocles."

"Does this Sophocles write about fools?" Terence asked bitterly.

"No," Acoriondes said. "But he does write about lies."

Without another word, Terence went back to finish his rough care of Bernard's wounds, while Acoriondes trussed Cligés and Fenice with ropes. The two lovers looked pathetically small, lying there together. And so they were, Terence thought.

12

Bringing All Things to Light

Guinglain was sitting in the grass of his yard, basking in the late-afternoon sun, when Terence rode into his clearing. Surprisingly, there were no children about. Terence had never been to Guinglain's hermitage without seeing a crowd of children. "I send them home for dinner," the young hermit said without moving. "They should be with their families. And besides, I don't have enough food." At last he opened his eyes and smiled. "I'm glad you're back," he said.

"I'm glad to see you, too," Terence replied, dismounting. As eager as he was to return to Arthur's court, he had ridden out of his way to stop at Guinglain's hut in the forest. Perhaps because he had been raised by a forest hermit very like the young Guinglain, Terence found his deepest peace with this friend. "I wasn't sure you'd even know I'd been gone."

"Oh, yes," Guinglain said. "I may live out of society here, but everyone in England knows about your journey to Greece." His eyes narrowed as he looked at Terence's face, and he raised one eyebrow. "But you've been farther than that, haven't you?"

Terence nodded but didn't elaborate. "What's been going on in England and Arthur's court?" he asked. He had been asking that question at every inn and village he had come to, but mostly he had heard tales of tournaments and feasts and spectacles — nothing of importance.

"Gawain returned from Greece a few months ago, bringing the sad news of Emperor Alexander's death. It was a great sorrow for the court, and for Lady Sarah especially." Terence nodded soberly, and Guinglain added, "Mordred is back, as well, bringing with him tales of great deeds done on the continent."

"Which no one else saw, I suppose," Terence murmured.

Guinglain only smiled. "It is said that the king is very pleased with young Mordred and honors him greatly. I know little more than that."

"And for all that you've said everything that I needed to know," Terence said.

Guinglain rose to his feet. "But now you must tell me your tale. Come inside and share my bread."

A few minutes later, having seen to his horse, Terence joined the hermit at a rough table by the fire.

There Guinglain said a quiet prayer, broke a loaf of brown bread and handed half to Terence, and poured him a cup of clear, cool water. Terence felt the simplicity of this home soaking into his being, like the warmth of a hot bath on a cold day, and began telling Guinglain all that had passed since their departure for the continent. Guinglain said nothing until Terence came to the discovery of Cligés and Fenice and the death of Alis. At that point, Terence paused.

After a moment, Guinglain asked, "Why do you stop?"

"It still makes me angry," Terence admitted. "It was all needless. Cligés and Fenice were children playing a game, pretending to be courtly lovers from a romance. But people were hurt, even killed, for their game."

"They aren't the only ones who play make-believe. Most people do, I would think."

Terence nodded. "Maybe you're right. After all, even Alexander played the courtly romance game when he was wooing Sarah. But behind his play-acting, Alexander really loved her. Cligés and Fenice — they had nothing but the game. All they had was pretense."

"What happened to the squire, Bernard?"

"He will live," Terence said. "With one leg, but he will live."

"I am glad. And Cligés and Fenice?"

"They live, too, but under lock and key. Acoriondes

couldn't bring himself to execute them, even for murdering Alis, but he couldn't let them go unpunished, either."

"Your friend Acoriondes is ruling the empire now?"

Terence nodded. "He's been declared regent until the legitimate heir can assume the throne." Guinglain raised a questioning eyebrow and Terence explained, "Fenice is pregnant."

Guinglain nodded slowly. "So the future emperor will be born in a prison."

"If you can call it a prison," Terence said. "Don't be imagining them in a dungeon. They have very comfortable rooms. Separate rooms."

"Separate. So Cligés and Fenice will never see each other again?"

"Not in truth," Terence replied. "But when did truth ever matter to them? Acoriondes made one more provision for them. In a nearby room he has also locked up the nurse Thessala, and he's given her the task of preparing her Elixer of Good Dreams for Cligés and Fenice. Every night they drink the potion, then go to sleep believing that they're in each other's arms."

An expression of deep sorrow settled on Guinglain's face. "How horrible," he murmured. "To spend the rest of your life locked away with nothing but your own lies."

Terence nodded. "That's their punishment."

"It's more than a punishment; it's a hell," Guinglain said, with feeling.

"I doubt they agree with you. After all, they've always preferred their lies. It may be a hell, but it's the hell they've always chosen."

"Everyone's hell is the one they choose. It's still horrible."

Terence wasn't sure he agreed, but he only repeated Sylvanus's words from Elysium: "Justice is often cruel."

Terence rode hard from Guinglain's hermitage and arrived at Camelot shortly after dark on the fourth day. The gates were closed, but the guard recognized Terence at once and raised the portcullis to let him in. Terence stabled his horse by feel in the pitch black stables, then turned eager eyes to the castle keep and smiled: a light showed at Eileen's window.

A minute later he was swinging through the window into Eileen's sitting room, where he found his love talking with Sarah by the fire. Seeing him, Eileen leaped to her feet, and then for several minutes there were no words. At last Eileen managed to say, in a muffled voice, "When did you get back?"

"Minutes ago."

"Have you seen anyone else?"

Terence shook his head. "I came here first."

Eileen took his hand. "Come sit with us."

Terence allowed himself to be led to the fire. "Sarah,

I'm glad to see you. I hadn't expected you to still be here."

"Actually," Sarah replied, "I'm here *again*. I went home for a while after we got word of Alexander's death, but it was lonelier at home than it used to be, so I came back."

Terence nodded. Sarah had spoken simply, and her matter-of-fact tone somehow spoke more truly of grief than tears would have. "I am sorry," Terence said simply. "He was a good man."

"Yes," Sarah replied. "He was. He was a man of honor and courage and joy and compassion. I didn't see it at first, being so annoyed at his minstrels and all that courtly love business, but in the end I realized that he never claimed to be anything but what he was. He was a rare man."

"You *did* love him," Terence said.

"I still do," Sarah replied calmly.

Eileen asked, "Did you ever find out who poisoned him?"

Terence hesitated only a second. "It was Mordred."

Both woman stared at him, eyes wide. At last Eileen said, "But why?"

"Spite," Terence said. It was what the Old One had said, and Terence had concluded that he — or perhaps she — had been correct. "Mordred had planned a civil war in Greece — partly to weaken Alexander and partly just to stir up trouble. When Alexander proved to be generous and wise and war was prevented, Mordred poisoned him on impulse. It's the only real weakness I've found in Mordred."

"But you know he's the murderer?" demanded Sarah.

"Yes."

"And you can prove it?"

Terence shook his head. "No. I have only the testimony of a blind seer in a land of shadows in a different world. In effect, I have certainty but not proof."

Eileen frowned. "But Mordred is . . . but tomorrow the king is calling all the court together to present Mordred to them."

"Present him? What do you mean? He's already been knighted."

"I know," Eileen said. "Kai thinks the king's going to reveal some secret, but he wouldn't say what. I believe Kai's sworn to silence. Do you know what he's talking about?"

Terence gazed blankly at the stone wall. So Arthur had at last convinced Guinevere to let him tell the secret of Mordred's birth. Once the court knew that Mordred was Arthur's son — illegitimate or not — he would be accepted as the heir to the throne. At that point, Mordred would be one murder away from ruling England.

"You *do* know, don't you? What is it?" Eileen demanded.

"I made the same vow Kai did," Terence said.

"Sorry. What does Gawain say? Does he think Kai's right?"

Eileen exchanged a glance with Sarah. "I couldn't say," she said. "I try to avoid Gawain these days."

Terence blinked with surprise. "Why? You aren't angry at him, are you?"

"No, it's not that. It's . . . well, do you remember that German chit who was here for a visit just before Alexander arrived? Venice or something like that?"

"Fenice," Terence said. "Yes, I remember her."

"Well, as you may recall, before she left she started the rumor that Gawain and I had been secret lovers for years. Now it's all over England. Minstrels are singing sickly songs about us."

Sarah almost smiled. "Sickly? How can you say so? I hear that Gawain has a picture of you that he carries with him everywhere, next to his heart. Not to mention the secret chapel he's had built in the forest, where he prays to your beauty. Did you know that he once killed a knight for saying that your features weren't perfect?"

"Really?" Terence asked. "Which features?"

"Never mind," Sarah replied primly.

"It's not funny, Terence," Eileen said. "It's an incredible pain in the . . . in the *features*. I can't have a normal conversation with any of the other ladies. Within five minutes, they're dropping hints about Gawain and giggling. And I think it's nearly as bad for Gawain. The older knights disapprove of him for carrying on a clandestine affair, and the young knights treat him like some kind of romantic hero. They say he's just like Sir Tristram."

"He must love that," Terence said.

"Anyway, Gawain and I agreed to stay away from each other for a while, to let the rumors die down. We haven't spoken in a month."

"Is it working?"

Eileen shrugged, but Sarah said, "Making things worse, more like. I think it's easier to invent stories about nothing at all than about a little. Gawain's been talking about going out on quest, just to get away, but he wanted to wait until you showed up."

"I'm glad he's still here," Terence said, his mind busy. "When is this ceremony supposed to take place tomorrow?"

"Midmorning," Eileen said.

Terence turned back toward the window. "Don't tell anyone that you've seen me," he said. Then he slipped out into the darkness. He had to run some errands before catching a few hours of sleep in the darkness of the stables.

The crowds were gathering in the Great Court as Terence dressed with care, making sure every buckle was secure before pulling a monk's cowl over his head. He had no real fear of being recognized under the long hood — he had deliberately borrowed his cowl from

Brother Albert, the tallest monk in the nearby Glaston-
bury Abbey — but neither did he see any need to show
himself earlier than necessary. He waited in the recesses
of the stable until he heard trumpets announcing the
king's arrival. Then he made his deliberate way into the
court, where the king was just beginning a speech to
the assembled crowd.

"My friends," King Arthur began, "I have called
you here today for a joyous occasion, but also one of
sorrow. I have, for these many years, ruled you under
the banners of truth and justice. I hope that I have been
just, but I have not always been truthful."

This stark introduction had the effect of silencing
the crowd. Knights, ladies, and courtiers looked uncertainly at one another, then back at the king. Behind
Arthur, Terence saw the grim, white visage of Queen
Guinevere. She may have given her permission for
Arthur to reveal his infidelity, but she clearly wasn't
happy about it.

"Sir Mordred!" called the king. "Come stand beside
me." Mordred disengaged himself from a knot of admirers near the king and stepped up to the king's right
hand. His face was a mask of innocent surprise. King
Arthur went on. "You have all heard of Sir Mordred's
deeds in Flanders and Bohemia. You know how he slew
the two-headed dragon of Prague and the four brothers
of Cassel. Moreover, even before his quest, you know
how he fought beside Emperor Alexander at the Battle

of Windsor and killed the rebel Count Anders with his own hand. Few knights have earned such acclaim so young."

Mordred's band of admirers, led by Agrivaine, burst into spontaneous applause. The king held up his hand for calm and, after a moment, continued. "Less impressive, but in many ways more admirable, is Mordred's ability to inspire others about him. He is a natural leader. My court has been blessed with many true heroes — Gawain, Lancelot, and others — but though heroes are rare, it is still rarer to find a hero who is also a leader of men. Mordred is such a hero."

Terence felt almost physically ill, but he kept his head down and continued to worm his way to the front.

"All this you have seen for yourselves," the king went on. "Thus far I have told you nothing new. But now I must reveal to you one more fact, unknown to you. Indeed, it is unknown to Mordred himself."

Mordred blinked and looked surprised, as Terence was sure he was not. Behind the king, Guinevere clenched her fists, then suddenly turned on her heel and hurried into the castle keep. King Arthur heard her footsteps and turned to see her disappear inside. His eyes were weary and strained, but his voice was steady as he continued.

"What I am about to say does not reflect well on me, and for that reason I have kept it hidden as long as I have. But to hide from truth is the greatest weakness of all. No wrong can ever be overcome by pretense, and lies can never serve the cause of good. Today I intend to reveal to you the whole truth, because partial truth looks too much like partial falsehood."

A low chuckle to Terence's right caught his ear, and something in the tenor of that voice made him look sharply toward its source. A bent old peasant woman, a basket of scrawny chickens in her arms, was watching the king with an expression of gleeful anticipation. Terence had never seen that face before, but her eyes were frighteningly familiar. Quickly he averted his own eyes before she should feel his gaze and look at him.

"Twenty years ago," King Arthur continued, "when I was new as a king, and newer still as a husband, I betrayed both my kingdom and my queen." Not a whisper of sound disturbed the courtyard. The crowd looked like so many brightly dressed statues. "Pretending that I was going off to pray, I used to put on borrowed armor and ride about challenging knights to joust with me. It seemed a harmless enough game to me, but as you will see, pretense is never harmless. While I was in disguise on one of these journeys, I came upon a young woman alone and seduced her."

There was a faint murmur from the crowd. The king allowed it to die down, then continued, "To take advantage of that woman was shameful. To hide the deed this many years was more shameful still. But I have been justly rebuked by a nobler example. Most of you know how Sir Mordred spoke openly about his own origins when he came to court, how his mother had been left with child by a wandering knight whose name he didn't even know."

The mutterings from the crowd grew louder as people began to realize what the king was saying. Arthur held up his hand, "And so, following the example of Sir Mordred, I reveal to you today that I was that wandering knight. Sir Mordred, you are my son. And now, at last, the full truth is revealed."

Even the murmurs stopped now, and in the stunned silence, Terence stepped forward and threw back the hood of his cowl. "Not the *full* truth, Your Highness. Not yet."

"Terence?" King Arthur said, gaping. Mordred whirled around and stared at Terence with undisguised hatred. Behind him, Terence heard a low growl from the old woman.

"You're right, O king," Terence continued, stepping closer. "A partial truth is a lot like a partial lie. You're right that you are Mordred's father. But you haven't told who his mother is."

King Arthur looked surprised, but his eyes grew suddenly wary and he cast a sharp glance at Mordred. "I don't know her name," the king said quietly.

"I do," Terence said, stepping between the king and Mordred and deliberately turning his back on the younger knight. "It isn't so hard to figure out, really.

All you have to do is ask who would be so devious as to purposely entrap the king. She did, you know. You may think that you seduced her, but in fact, you were ensnared by a lying doxy."

"How dare you!" roared Mordred, behind Terence. "To speak so of my dead mother!"

Terence didn't even look over his shoulder. "Oh, she's not dead. That was just one of your lies. In fact, if I had to guess, I'd say that that the trollope wasn't far away, to watch her enemy's fall." Arthur's eyes widened, and Terence said, "That's right, sire. Mordred's mother is the enchantress who has tried so many times to destroy you, none other than —"

Terence sensed rather than saw the movement behind him, and he tensed his back and braced his feet. Mordred's dagger thumped heavily against his back, but Terence only staggered a couple of steps before turning around and facing the livid Mordred, who gasped, "You . . . but I . . . how did you?"

"I'm wearing chain mail," Terence said calmly. "I only wish Bedivere had done the same."

With a cry of inhuman fury Mordred flung himself at Terence, who slipped easily through his arms. Terence wore a small dagger at his own side, but in the loose robes it might as well have been back in Greece. Instead he concentrated on evading Mordred's flashing dagger. Three times Mordred slashed at Terence, each time aiming at the head or throat, and three times Terence dodged the blow. When Mordred tried a fourth time, though, the dagger was knocked flying from his hand by two long swords that reached in from opposite sides and struck at nearly the same moment. Terence didn't even have to look to know who his rescuers were: he knew both swords by sight. Both were faery-made blades: Gawain's Sword Galatine and Arthur's Excalibur.

"I'm sorry, Your Highness," Terence said. "But it is true. Your only son is also the son of the enchantress Morgause, your greatest enemy. He was conceived and raised for no other purpose than to destroy your kingdom."

"Sleep!" came a shrill shout from the crowd. Terence turned to see the old woman with the basket of chickens raise herself up to her full height and before their eyes assume the majestic form of Morgause herself. She held one hand in the air, and all around her people began to drop to the ground in charmed sleep. Gawain and Arthur both sagged, but Terence felt as awake as ever and caught Galatine before Gawain fell to the ground. In a moment only two figures remained standing: Morgause with her upraised arm and Terence, standing guard over the king.

"You have been bothersome again, squire," Morgause hissed. "Do you think you can save Arthur forever?"

"I know nothing about forever," Terence said. "But I can save him this time. It's what I do, you know."

At that moment a small hand, like that of a child, rested on Terence's forearm, and he glanced down into the face of his friend Robin. "Hallo, lad," the elf said. "Miss me?"

"Where've you been?" Terence asked, his eyes flickering back to Morgause.

"Hanging about. But you've set us free from the Lady's spell," Robin said. "You and the king there, I mean. Her enchantments are crumbling." Then there were others with Robin, austere ladies and grinning sprites, all from the Seelie Court of the Noble Faeries.

Morgause uttered a shriek of frustration and shouted, "Come to us, my knight!" A knight on horseback stormed through the open castle gates and rode up to where they stood. Leaning low from the saddle, he took Mordred by the collar and hauled him up over the pommel of the saddle. Morgause leaped lightly up behind him, and a moment later the three were gone.

"You're just letting them go?" Terence complained to Robin.

"Don't worry," the imp said reassuringly. "I'm sure they'll be back."

"That wasn't exactly what I . . . Never mind," Terence said. In truth, he didn't know what he would do with Morgause if he had her prisoner anyway.

"The others will be waking up in a moment," Robin said. "We'll be off. Nicely done, today, your grace."

Then Terence was left, the sole standing figure in

Camelot's Great Court. A moan came from his feet, and he saw Gawain stirring and rubbing his eyes. Terence returned his sword. "Here, milord. Thanks kindly."

It took nearly twenty minutes for everyone to be fully awake again, and then another half-hour for Terence to explain again how Morgause had seduced the king by enchantment so many years before, all as part of a deeply laid plot against his throne. Then he had to explain before everyone how Mordred had been behind every plot and rebellion and murder of the past months. The crowd of Mordred's admirers clearly hated hearing all this — Agrivaine's expression was positively venomous — but having seen Mordred lose control and try to stab Terence in the back, there was little anyone could say in his defense. Arthur seemed to grow grayer and older at each new revelation of his son's perfidy, but when Terence finished his speech, the king's voice was strong. "Terence, again I thank you. A little while ago, I called for truth; now I suppose I have to accept it."

"Your Highness?" Terence said. "You were right. There's no virtue in pretense. And with your permission, I would like to reveal a lie of my own."

"You? A lie?" the king stammered, blinking.

"Yes, sire. For many years now I have loved a noble lady, have even pledged myself to her and vowed to be faithful, but I have kept that love hidden."

"Why?" asked the king.

"Because I'm just a squire, and she's a noblewoman.

If it were known that she loved one so far beneath her, she'd be scorned."

"Terence, if any woman was ashamed of your love —" the king began.

"It wasn't her, sire. She's never asked for secrecy. I was the one who insisted on it. But I don't want to love in secret anymore." Terence turned in a circle, scanning the crowd for Eileen. At last Gawain nudged him and pointed to a window in the castle keep, just above their heads. "There you are," Terence said. "Eileen, would you marry me? In public this time, I mean."

Eileen lifted her chin and spoke in a ringing voice. "Of course I will, you ass, and if I might speak a bit of truth myself, it's about bleeding time, you blithering lackwit!"

Terence felt himself grinning foolishly, and he started for the stairs to go to her, but the king's hand dropped heavily on his shoulder. "One moment, Terence. There is one more pretense to clear up." Turning to the assembled crowd, King Arthur raised his voice in a shout. "Not for another second will I permit my friend and protector Squire Terence to pretend that he is a mere squire, or a mere anything! There is no knight in my kingdom to whom I owe more! Terence! On your knees!"

Terence hesitated, confused.

"Now, Terence!" roared Arthur. "Your king has given you a command, by God!"

271

Terence dropped to his knees, and King Arthur raised the Sword Excalibur, then touched the flat of the blade on Terence's head and shoulders. "Today I make a knight. No, today I recognize as knight one who has been one for years. Rise, Sir Terence, and be known as a fellow of the Round Table. Be ever true to your God; protect always your neighbor; honor always your king."

Terence stood uncertainly, only vaguely aware of the cheers of the court. He was looking up into the smiling eyes of his Eileen. But behind him he could just make out Gawain's voice muttering, "Damn. Does this mean I have to polish my own armor?"

Author's Note

One of the most important — if not always the best — of the Arthurian storytellers was the French poet Chrétien de Troyes. Chrétien lived and wrote in the twelfth century, in Champagne, where he was fortunate enough to have a patroness—the noble Marie de Champagne—who paid his bills even when he churned out a stinker, which sometimes happened.

Chrétien's tales were sometimes very good (like his *Yvain*) and sometimes very bad (like his *Knight of the Cart*). Some of them were never finished (*Perceval*) and others were misplaced entirely (such as his telling of the Tristram and Iseult story). But whatever else they were, Chrétien's stories were influential. Chrétien changed the world of Arthurian legend forever. He was the one who made the stories as much about love

as about adventure. You could almost say that Chrétien was the inventor of the love story.

But what a love Chrétien's "courtly love" was! In his
tales, knights swore eternal faithfulness to their mistresses — rather than to, for instance, their wives —
and their mistresses ruled these lovesick knights with
an iron hand. Also, nearly all the Arthurian love stories end tragically. For some reason, it was considered
romantic to die for love. Not half-witted: romantic.

Of Chrétien's love stories, perhaps the least known
is his *Cligés,* which forms the skeleton of this book.
Chrétien's version, like my own, is divided in half. Part
One deals with the love of Emperor Alexander, and
the second part with Cligés and Fenice. All the most
outlandish parts of this book were borrowed directly
from Chrétien, including Thessala's Potion of Good
Dreams, Fenice's fake death, and Cligés's double en-
tombment.

Retelling *Cligés* has also given me a chance to explore
a part of the Middle Ages that is often ignored: the
Byzantine Empire. This proud empire, with its capital
at Constantinople (now Istanbul, Turkey), was the direct descendant of the ancient Roman Empire. While
Byzantium was nowhere near as strong as ancient Rome,
it was still a formidable power, with its own traditions,
its own preferred language (Greek, rather than Latin),
and even its own distinct style of church. Such a tradition certainly deserves to be studied.

However, you'll have to do that on your own. What you'll learn about the empire in this book is neither very complete nor very accurate. The problem is that my source, Chrétien, wasn't very complete or accurate himself, and I had to choose whether to be faithful to history or faithful to my story.

Given that choice, I'll take the story every time. Historical accuracy isn't the point in Arthurian romances anyway. The few historical details that do appear in them are like bits of meat tossed into the fictional soup for flavoring. In the end, it all cooks together, and we swallow the whole dish. Just pretend it's historical, all right? And maybe you'll find something in the story that's *real*, which is not at all the same thing as *accurate* — and usually much better.

— Gerald Morris